Péter Nádas

LOVE

TRANSLATED FROM THE HUNGARIAN BY
Imre Goldstein

VINTAGE

Published by Vintage 2001

2 4 6 8 10 9 7 5 3 1

Copyright © Péter Nádas 1979

Translated from the Hungarian by Imre Goldstein
Translation copyright © Farrar, Straus and Giroux, Inc. 2000

First published in Great Britain in 2001 by
Jonathan Cape

First published in 1979 by Szépirodalmi Könyvkiadó,
Budapest, Hungary, as *Szerelem*

Vintage
Random House, 20 Vauxhall Bridge Road,
London SW1V 2SA

Random House Australia (Pty) Limited
20 Alfred Street, Milsons Point, Sydney
New South Wales 2061, Australia

Random House New Zealand Limited
18 Poland Road, Glenfield, Auckland 10,
New Zealand

Random House (Pty) Limited
Endulini, 5A Jubilee Road, Parktown 2193,
South Africa

The Random House Group Limited Reg. No. 954009
www.randomhouse.co.uk

A CIP catalogue record for this book
is available from the British Library

ISBN 0 09 928649 1

Printed and bound in Great Britain by
Bookmarque Ltd, Croydon, Surrey

LOVE

"Gimme a pillow."

She stands up. Dark foyer behind the glass-paned open door. She leaves the room. I close my eyes. Beyond the room, outside, the small bell of the church clock strikes once, twice. I try to imagine how it sits in space. And also the street, and the church wedged in tightly between the houses across the street. Its tower, rising above the roofs, against the city sky glimmering in reflected neon lights. The house whose top floor I walked up to. The staircase. The apartment on the top floor. The room, the bed. The bed in which I am lying. Some time goes by. I hear the click of the door. She closed it. A plop: the pillow thrown on the bed. I open my eyes. She goes back to the table. I stuff the big pillow under me so that, if she decides to lie down next to me, she'll have plenty of room. She sits down at the table. Like this, with the pillow under my back, I am very comfortable; the comfort of the moment. I can feast my eyes on her. The familiar forms of her

3

body in a green dress. Crackle of cellophane wrapping, she pulls a filter cigarette out of the pack, careful not to bruise the thin paper, picking at the tobacco with a matchstick. The tobacco spills out onto a sheet of paper; it's so quiet one can hear the sound it makes. We've already smoked one, sitting at the table.

At the table I was sitting in the armchair, half naked. All the paraphernalia on the table. A pack of cigarettes. Grass in a small plastic bag. Scissors, matches. A sheet of clean paper. She takes a cigarette out of the pack, then a matchstick from the matchbox. With the match she scoops out the tobacco, careful not to graze the fine paper shell of the cigarette. I am not leaning back. My shirt is on the backrest of the armchair, her green dress spread out over my shirt. She likes to walk around naked; it's hot. The tobacco is spilled out on the sheet of paper. Her breasts tremble imperceptibly, following with a slight delay the rhythm of her movements; the nipples touch the edge of the table. It's good to watch her working like this. When the hull is almost empty, she stands it up in front of her; it rests firmly on its filter base. She leans over it; her nipples get dented by the table's edge. Pinching a bit of grass from the plastic bag, she carefully stuffs it into the hull. Then she takes some regular tobacco, squeezing it between three of her fingers, but the hollowed-out cigarette tips over. She stands it up again. She pours the tobacco into it, adding a dash of grass from the plastic bag. She is packing it all down with the phosphorous end of the matchstick. "Aren't you thirsty?" she asks. A bit more tobacco, some more grass, and finally a few more strands of tobacco, packing it tight with the rounded end of the match. "I'll

4

get you some. In a minute." She rolls the cigarette shell, filled with layers of tobacco and grass, between her palms. She cuts the filter off with the scissors. She looks up, at me. "Gimme my dress." I reach for the green dress. "What for?" She stands up. "People can see into the kitchen." She lifts the dress over her head, the white groove of the scar on her belly tightens, her waist grows narrower, she slips into the dress. I lean back. She leaves the room. From here, from this armchair, the room can be seen really well. The door to the balcony is open.

I step out on the balcony. It's a little cooler out here. The narrow little street, down in the depths, is empty and dark. All the shadows are in their appropriate places. Actually, I should come right out and say that I won't be coming back here anymore. Some time goes by. The cavernous portal of the church appears to be leading to an underground canal full of sewage water. I know I won't tell her; she is so unsuspecting, I can't do it. I turn around. She is standing in the middle of the room, and I haven't even heard her come back. She is holding two glasses as she stands under the antique chandelier. Lovely. "Doesn't this balcony get on your nerves?" She laughs. Her eyes disappear in the laughter. "I never go out on it!" "This railing is too low not to tempt one into thinking." "About leaping over it, is that what you mean? I never step out on it! I'd open the door, but I've never been out there." "Never?" "Yes. I'm pretty sure, never." I take one of the glasses from her. Lemonade. I drink. I go back and sit down in the armchair, put the glass on the table, it makes a little clinking sound. Talking about such far-fetched things doesn't seem to work. Maybe it's better when we talk about nothing in particular. She sits down, facing me, but only at the edge of her chair. She picks up the cigarette, puts it between her lips, and quickly lights up. Too bad, I would have liked us to smoke it while lying in bed. She takes a puff, swallowing the smoke deep into herself. Nothing of the smoke should be wasted. She hands it over. I take a powerful drag. In my mouth, in my throat, the taste is familiar. I'm trying to swallow it as deep as I can. I've an urge to cough; I hand it back to her; she's taking her turn; but I mustn't cough. If I did, I'd waste it all. I close my eyes and imagine, I can feel, the small sacs of my lungs filling up. She coughs and gives back the joint. I have to open my eyes. The joint's burning too fast. I draw hard, it sputters. The smoke rises freely. I bend over it, trying to take it in with my nostrils as well. I'd give the joint to her, but she motions she doesn't want it just now. I get to take two drags. Women know how to make tasty food. The lungs are getting full, they're drinking hard. Slowly I'd let out what's left over, but there is nothing left over. Another pull and I hand it to her. I'd like to lie down on the bed, there to wait for it to happen. I get the joint again. This is the end of it; two, maybe three puffs left in it. The heat of the red ashes on my fingers, and so much smoke is going to waste. I hand it back again, carefully, so she won't burn her hand or my fingers. She sucks on it with her eyes closed; the tiny embers must be burning her lips. A wrong gift. I get up. Take off my pants, throw them on the armchair. Nothing yet. She squashes the roach in the ashtray and coughs out what's left of the smoke. "Would you mind giving me a sheet? I'd like to lie down." She gets up. Steps over to the chest of drawers. On its top, among books, newspapers, and magazines, a kitchen alarm is ticking. She pulls out a drawer, I take the sheet. She shoves the drawer home, it squeaks. I spread the sheet over the bed. I lie down. Where I usually do. Pressing my head and shoulders against the wall, as I usually do. She goes back to the table, sits down. "I'll get the next one ready. All right?" "All right." In the lovely light of the chandelier; lovely chandelier; I'd like to withdraw from it; in general, I'd like to withdraw from everything. "Would you mind turning off the light?" She gets up. Walks past the chest of drawers, to the switch. She turns off the light. A wall lamp above me is lit. It's uncomfortable like this, the wall is pressing my shoulders, and the wallpaper is pricking my skin. She seems ready to sit back down at the table. The unpleasantness of bodily sensations may be reduced by comfort. She sits down. "Gimme a pillow."

She stands up. Dark foyer behind the glass-paned open door. She leaves the room. I've never taken a good look inside the foyer. Is that where they keep the bedding? I close my eyes. The door should be closed so we'd be left to ourselves. Outside, some-where above my head, the church bell is tolling. I try to imag-ine my place in space. Room on the seventh floor. Some time goes by before I hear the clicking of the door. She has shut it. The pillow thrown on the bed makes a gentle thud. I open my eyes. I stuff the big pillow under me, but not all of it, so she can have some of the pillow in case she decides to lie down next to me. She sits down at the table. From here, from the bed, every-thing can be seen very well. She sits right in the center of my field of vision. The familiar forms of her body in a green dress. Crackle of cellophane wrapping, she pulls a cigarette out of the

pack, careful not to bruise the thin paper; picking at the tobacco with a matchstick. The tobacco spills out onto a sheet of
paper; it's so quiet one can hear the sound it makes. Nothing
unusual, yet. Everything is as it should be. She sits at the table,
where we've already smoked one. Out on the street a car bar-
rels by. I feel that if I let fatigue take over I'll fall asleep, and that
wouldn't be good. The whole thing would be wasted, I'd sleep
through its effect. Or maybe it would be working on me in the
depths of my dreams, but I'm fed up with my dreams, too. It's
hot in the room. Even though the window above the bed is
open. And the door to the balcony is also open, as is the other
window; I'd like to take off my underpants, they're making me
sweat, but it would bother me to lie like this, with my legs
spread out, naked. I don't want to see my own body. A hefty
folder containing a manuscript is on the radiator. I've got to
read it tomorrow; in fact, I should have read it today, or yesterday, because today might be tomorrow already. My watch is on
top of the folder, I could take a look at it and check whether
what we've got here is yesterday or tomorrow, but this movement would surely upset the inner apathy I'm still waiting for.
Next to my watch an ashtray, a pack of cigarettes, and matches.
I could have a smoke. It seems that the calmness that leads to
apathy is impossible to achieve. "Would I upset the ritual if I
had a smoke?" I've got to kill time with something, with either
some movement or some thought. "Wait, right away. I'm
bringing it right away." So, to wait. She pinches a bit of grass
from the plastic bag, working slowly, calmly. "D'you feel anything?" Her voice is full, belonging to her body. "No. Nothing.
I'm just tired. And you?" "Nothing." Her movements are full,

8

too; she is all calm concentration: whatever she needs to do should be done well, every single gesture executed without the tension of single-minded resolve. It's as if she were alone in the room, as if I weren't here at all; I've never seen her so artlessly peaceful. And it's as if I am the same way, too. As if the cramps of concentration had floated out of me. This is a state not of concentration but of seeing. The sight before me is not something I'm explaining but something simply reaching me untouched. And what has reached me, untouched, is she. She rolls the restuffed cigarette shell between her palms. Her full brown arms in the cut of the green dress. Her flesh seems fleshier. The table, too, seems to be farther from the bed. Accessibly far away. If she comes over I'll feel her skin on mine. Waiting is a good dimension, one can find in it at once what is and what isn't possible, the unimaginable and the imaginable. We will be making love, all right. Indifference includes everything. Distance between two points. One point, a self-reliant body, there, at the table, a female figure; I am attracted to her because I am the other point, lying here, with the hair on my leg showing, thighs spread apart, cambered protuberance covered with underpants; but this distance can be reduced. The body is laughable, fallible, ridiculously simple; I could take off my underpants, they're superfluous. But if that is what I think of the superfluousness of movements, then something must have started. Indifference, in which I see the world around me in a sharper relief, because I have ceased checking everything. Indifference is the completeness of *is* without *was* and *may be*. She picks up the scissors, cuts off the filter. "D'you feel anything?" The filter plops on the tabletop. "Maybe. And you?" "Yes, I do. Like it's beginning."

stands up. Coming toward the bed. The joint in her hand. Across the distance. She hesitates. "Yes, I can see it! by the way you move!" She draws her palm across her forehead, smiling. "Yes. But not much yet." She passes out of the frame. I should turn to follow her. The bed sinks under me; she's sat down. She puts the joint on the night table. Among other objects. Tape recorder. Book. Telephone. Lemonade in a glass, which she did not drink. Her barely perceptible smile becomes weighty and meaningful, taking me along, making me smile, driving me toward a halcyon border beyond which, I can feel it, there is nothing except infinite smiling. Still, it is frightening, I should run away. The smile is opening within me; it is a distance that is not outside of me but in me, yet it is infinite. Infinite means the final settling of accounts. The one you've longed for! Which, nevertheless, is still frightening now. But I don't want it, I don't want anything, I don't want to defend myself. I am looking at her. Her smile is an object, it could penetrate me, can break up distances; she'll be mine, if I let her, though there is still some real distance between us. But I don't stretch out my arm. This is external distance, and she is smiling to herself in an inner distance, for herself, not for me. Still, even in this way, she is mine. She stirs. She turns around, pulls her legs up on the bed, her back against the wall, but not on the pillow where I left room for her. She wants to be far from me, but even like this she is close. Within her own comfort, within me. Now is the time when I should draw her to myself, while we are inseparable in our mutual sensation of each other; I should get her on her back now and take her dress off. She's got her panties on; and

I'm still in my underpants. These imagined movements are much too complicated to be carried out. I turn my head away. White, distant white. At the edge of my frame of vision is the open door of the balcony, with the reflections of the glass panes. It's good like this. This is no longer waiting. Everything is good now. Maybe we shouldn't even smoke another one. Objects in the softened silence. Bookcase, open balcony door, white wall. A hand appears in the picture, her hand. It's as if for a long time I'd forgotten she's here, beside me. The cigarette in her hand. As if I'd forgotten about my own presence as well; I have become what I have seen, for a long time, which was probably a very short time. Was. I should open my mouth! I do. She puts it between my lips, the hand covers the action, I bring my lips together. My arm is resting by my side. A palm and spread fingers on the white sheet, above me the wall lamp in its own yellowish light. She leans over me, a clear face dressed in a gentle smile. She gives me a light. I can hear the match strik-ing, but from farther away, from a distance greater than the one from which I can see it. I have to get hold of the cigarette, be-cause my mouth has no strength. I raise my hand and get hold of it, the way it should be done. It catches on, I inhale, its tip glows. Yes, this is it, the real taste. It's choking me. Wants to make me cough. If I did, the smoke would go to waste. I hand it over. To swallow the smoke as deep as possible, hold it in for a long time. The depth to which I can inhale the smoke seems deeper now. Her long lashes are lowered. Her lids are filled out, like her body, and her voice, too. It's pleasant to watch her in-hale; to see, between her eyebrows, the lines of concentration, in the sleeveless green dress the rising shoulders that stiffen when she inhales. To press her to myself. Not the body, but that concentration and attention directed to herself, to make that mine. But first let's finish smoking. Her lashes are rising; her blue, very blue eyes in the yellowish light of the wall lamp. Unsmiling. The smoke making her cough; she grasps her throat, her body writhing, bends her head, struggling, coughing. I take the joint from her. I am smoking it but I can't feel that I am, I can only see that I'm inhaling; what I sense now is not the usual sensation, not the joy of smoking or the gesture of holding the joint; it's not the hollow of the mouth that begs for the smoke. It is in the tiny sacs of the lungs where desire sits, joylessly but very greedily, in my chest, down there; as if that were the lowest, most important spot of the body, where this desire to be gratified is now nesting. In the inhaling. In, in, everything must be taken in. I'd give it back to her, but she motions she doesn't want it. The two extreme points of the great distance are now within me, inside. Between the mouth and the lungs. The distance: desire. Quickly I let out what's left, to make room for the fresh smoke, so there will be only inhaling, to reach the point of overcoming distance, which is desire. I take a drag. Deeper. But desire recedes even deeper. Her hand places an ashtray between my spread thighs. It is round, made of copper, full of ashes and butts, now on the white sheet in front of me. I bend over it. I draw and drag, inhaling deeper, but it's no use; there is something deeper than deep itself, I can't get any deeper, no matter how much I bend over, the movement cannot reduce the inner distance. Even with my nose I am swallowing. The smoke is floating freely and would go to waste; I am swallowing it even with my nose. But the distance is growing. Insatiable. The amount of smoke increases it even more. I straighten out. I'd give it back to her, but she motions she doesn't want it, I should keep on smoking. She's looking at me. This is not a look of suspicion, not the old look. Neutral. As if looking at an object. It doesn't bother me. I might as well be an object. I take another puff, the hot ashes part from the body of the joint and fall into the ashtray. A live ember. With the extinguished end of the joint I skewer the ember. I take a drag. The ember rejoins and blends into the body of the joint, giving out a dense smoke. I hand it over. She takes it. Her lids are lowered, the lines of concentration crimp her eyebrows. Ugly. She hands it back, her face smooths into a smile, beautiful. I am smoking, but I can no longer inhale so deeply. I don't want it anymore.

"Don't throw it away!"

I give it back to her.

Everything is expanding, opening up. If I let it, it would expand into infinity. This is not yet infinity itself but an expansion into infinity

"You!"

I'd like to say something; there's something I'd like to tell you, but I can't because of this laughter

"You!"

I simply must laugh at something; what is this all-fulfilling laughter from which I cannot extricate myself? I cannot get to the surface, from someplace down there; it clashes over my head, it emanates from me, and I can hear my own wild and coarse laughter, and I can feel my mouth, ajar and stretched toward the edges, from which this guffaw is issuing; inside, it has already conquered everything, everything that I am; I didn't want to say anything else except that it's my own witless laughter that makes me disgusting and idiotic, and all that because I wanted to say something

to you

but in the meantime I forgot what; what I did want to say has become one with me, so much so that now there's no need to say it; oh, I can't stand this laughing anymore, I'm choking, but that's laughable, too; it's never going to end, laughing is what makes me laugh, I can't stand it anymore! Now it's bursting forth from even deeper, it's even stronger, right out of my mouth, I can hear it. I shouldn't be doing this! And actually why not? That makes me laugh, too: having thoughts! Frighteningly superfluous, everything is good and superfluous.

With her eyes closed

she is lying on her back. It's quiet. That means that this whole laughing business is something I've only imagined. And my eyes must have been closed, because I didn't see anything, only the bursting, approaching, and receding waves of my imaginary laughter. I quickly slide my whole body farther down in the bed. My head off the wall and onto the pillow. The ashtray is not between my thighs anymore. I close my legs, just to be doing something against this laughter. Maybe the whole thing lasted but a few seconds. There's no way of checking it. In the meantime, she took away the ashtray. It's all right. Why am I constantly on the defensive, against everything? I stretch out my arm. She stirs, rolls over. The weight of her body makes me feel my own body. She snuggles into place, lays her face on my chest, throws an arm around me, locks my knee into her thighs. I see mostly green; this dress is really beginning to bother me. "Take this thing off!"

Without opening her eyes, she lifts herself up.

"Yes."

Her voice is but a resounding willingness that clings to my body. As if she herself no longer existed, except for me; for my sake, so that she could manifest herself in me. Her two well-shaped arms cross each other, and with her fingers she smartly grabs the hem of the dress and pulls it upward. The tanned mound of her belly is cut diagonally by the whiter stripe of her scar; the waist grows slimmer in the stretching, and then her white breasts bounce forward, these breasts untouched by sunshine, with their purplish areolae around the nipples. My mouth would like to reach up, but I make no move. It's not the body I need but the movement: the sight, the spectacle, just like this; if I restrain myself, deny myself the sensation of the body, then she is completely mine. I have never felt that even a movement made by someone else can be made my own. I close my eyes, looking up at what has become my possession. But without seeing it, I am free-falling into my own distances. Her thighs are locking themselves around my knee, drawing it toward her.

"Boy, I've got it made, boy, have I got it made!"

and

this voice, using my ears as a conduit, fills the body which is mine and whose integument I feel because of the weight of her clinging body. I can feel myself only, that's right, only if I feel her. This makes me happy. I put my arm around her. I have never felt her so much to be mine. She is squeezing me. I'm squeezing her. And once again as a voice she bursts into me through my ear.

"Hey! holy fuck, I feel good, boy do I feel good, I feel so goddamn good! Could I—boy, I feel so good—could I, could I tell you a little tale, could I, could I tale you a little tell? I'd love to tale you little tellings. Could I tell you, could I?"

and she is laughing. Her laughter fills me, and it pokes at, and also liberates, my own laughter, I can feel it, her voice is rolling in through my ear, and I could answer with the explosion of my own laughter; we are laughing, and it's no longer possible to separate our voices because they have blended, got thoroughly mixed up in each other, everything that would separate us has simply ceased, the only thing that's left is the threat of these sounds, all-encompassing, all-fulfilling, erupting and always rolling back. We should get hold of something that's outside all this. "Go ahead, tell me!" I hear the shouting of my own voice, and I know that I've thrust my own voice above the sound of laughter.

"Tell me! But the word you used before, don't say it, not that word, not now, not that kind of word, not now!"

She is not laughing anymore. Silence. I can feel it, I can feel how the absence of her laughter is streaming into me through my ear, so fully, exactly the way I felt the sounds of her voice; and the silence is growing ever longer, stretching, ever colder; it's my fault! because I am still checking things out; measuring morality in the midst of amorality, ridiculous! but the spoken sentence is irrevocable; just as what I am is irrevocable, because this is what I am, and although it bothers me, she cannot be altered either; but if I keep thinking about this, no I don't want to, because she is getting away from me and I'd like to get back to her; I cannot feel her body, nor her weight, though I know she is here; it was a bad sentence, one that has exposed me, and here I am plunging back into my own remoteness, I have lost her, even though it is

her

that I

want; how keenly, and strangely I am able to think just now, even if I feel nothing at all of what we call the outside world; I don't want that! these are my own thoughts, I don't want that! what I need is something to clutch at, something that could return me to her

"Tell me! Please. Go on, tell me!"

I hear my own voice, and I know that it was my own voice I could clutch at; and I can already see: her face on my shoulder, her closed eyelids, the teeth that flash in her laughter and glitter in her saliva, and I can hear her laughing. "Tell me! Please!" Her laughter fills out my body, all the way down to my toes, and the light weight of her body makes me feel the weight of my own, I can feel that I have a body; I am laughing, and I can hear my own laughter, separately. "Shall I tell you a little tale?" "Tell me!" We can't get out of it, even though she is ready to tell me; alarmingly we sink deeper into our hopelessly entangled shared happiness; a black moldable mass; suddenly I am torn from it by her squealing, girlish voice

croaky

croaky

what you say?

croak I

coax you

come away!

under the water, come

if you love me

the weather

down there is

never rainy

I know that this voice should cause physical pain, but there is nothing here that could feel any pain: both body and pain are but uncertain memories; still, some sort of pain or fear is present in that this laughter is un-stoppable, that perhaps from now on we must always go on laughing. Now I want to, I want to, me too! "Now I want to, I want to, me too!" I yell, but I don't know what I want. "Tell me! Terrific, wow, terrific! Tell me! You hear me? Tell me! Terrific, great, tell me!" she shrieks. "Now I want to!" I yell, I hear my own yelling, but it's not in my voice, it's somebody else's, it's that old voice, the voice of a child, and then her squealing is also that of the little girl she used to be

The little sparrow farted so hard

it

broke a leg

        and found itself in a hotel bed

                        I can't, I can't anymore, this laughing is too much; I should hold on to something, but what? should hold it back so I could continue; continue the story, and then we might laugh even louder, even harder

     with a thorn stuck up his ass!

                itsy-bitsy Quincy

                       you are

it-sy and you are out!

        out

         out

           receding, slowly the last word is receding

     out

        but laughter washes it away; now the laughter is no longer frightening, it's pleasant; a light ascent, and a protective shell that surrounds me with its cheerful soft heat, and I also know that I am lying here in the middle of this shell

                     with her, in her body, as if I had penetrated her body, without touching her body and without being touched; as if I were hovering inside her body, though I know I am not; I am only lying here, impossible, look, I still have my underpants on! and still, it is as if we

    might be getting closer

          just as we

              are getting away from the

uttered words, we are receding, and the same way something is approaching, a gentle frontier which we have once before experienced, and beyond this frontier this unsurpassably good state in which I now seem to be hovering motionless, yes, in her I am hovering, but in there this unsurpassable good flows over, yes it could overflow; this laughter-filled and gently hovering yelling increases to the level of a desperate scream, becoming the distance between two points; I am coming closer and closer

"Boy, is that good! Boy oh boy! Did you make that up yourself? I'm right, aren't I? you did it on the spot, didn't you? Terrific, oh boy! You made that up yourself, didn't you? It's good."

yes, it's good, really it is; I'd like to tell her that it's good, because always at the last moment, as if at the last moment your voice would yank me back, your voice won't let me get to the point which I always feel I am approaching, or is it the point that's coming toward me? I should tell her that no, I wasn't the one who made it up, but the little girl in the garden while raising one of her legs and jumping about

she was the one who said it in the garden

but it would be too long and complicated to say all that

"Yes. I made that up."

later I tell her that the little girl in the garden

"Do you know where I am? Right now I am seeing folk motifs. Folk motifs. I can see them. But I don't know where I am, I see only folk motifs and they seem to be, it's like I'm among folk motifs."

yes, folk motifs! her resonant voice with these folk motifs is now reviving folk motifs in me as well, or maybe just their memories? I'd like to tell her that I have also seen, not so long ago they have crossed my mind, too, or maybe I have actually seen such folk motifs; maybe it was yesterday, or today, or much longer ago, and I have to tell her that, because if this is so, if there is the kind of identification that can project one of my visual memories for her eyes to see, if there is such a power, then it must be the same folk motifs I've seen that have wound up in her head; it must be some sort of spilling over, it's not impossible; but I can't remember, as if there had never been anything that I could remember, except that there are two familiar words here, past and remembrance, that indicate that I did have a past, for words do mean something, and if I were able to remember, then at a specified point somewhere in that past would appear those folk motifs that have now been transferred to her head. But I can't recall what it is I should tell her, only that there is something that I should say about some folk motifs, of which I cannot remember what it is that I should tell her. But I must tell her! In this tension

I

feel

that I have thrust away from myself the body that has been lying on mine, and only now do I feel that her body had been lying on my body, something which I haven't felt until now: its weight; and I can also see it, which means that until now, without seeing anything—my eyes must have been closed—I was

2 1

only struggling with something, but did not feel it,

                                                        it seems
we're in this together,

                        but now I'm out of her, because I can see
and feel her; she's clutching my knee with her thighs, her arm's
around my shoulder, her head on my breast, I feel her face, the
heat of her body, its feverish fire, and it's as if I were also suffering from a high temperature, from a febrile fiery daze, from an
illness, or we may have made love, that's why this feverish grat-
ification,

       and the room

                     the furniture, the silence, and the white
wall opposite me all emerging from a dim torpor

                                         but no! this
only resembles the state that follows lovemaking; her head is on
my chest! then I must not have thrust her away, after all; she is
smiling on my chest. I probably shoved myself away from
something, from my own thoughts, which must have been hovering around some folk motifs; now her eyes are open, and this
smile that clearly says, You! "Are you in it now?" "I think I am,
yes!" Then! "Then try to come out of it, because I'd like to tell
you something interesting, and I'd like you to understand it
fully. About those folk motifs. You probably saw those folk motifs because I also did, hours ago, or yesterday, or I don't know
when, because it's like outside this moment, yes, outside this
one, the one in which I'm saying these very words, because I
am talking, am I not? it's as if nothing exists outside this moment. So what I'm saying is that I can't catch up with what was
somewhere in the past, but I believe you have taken those from
me."

"What have I taken from you?"

"Those folk motifs, that's what! You got them from me."

Placing one palm on my chest she raises herself above me; her other arm slips out from under my back. She stares at me. "What folk motifs?"

"The ones you were talking about!"

"And those I took from you?"

"Yes. I meant to give them to you, that's why you just sort of took them over from me."

She is staring at me and her smile is transformed into a smirk.

"But I think, I do think, dear, that we should not get out of it. We ought to give ourselves over to it, completely."

"All right. You're right." She's right, we ought to give ourselves over completely. Everything has its own rules. It should not be avoided; but if now, I mean just now, we did get out of it, then where did this confusing stuff come from? what folk motifs? This must be some kind of obsession. I didn't get out of it, I only thought I was sober; everything I feel is an illusion; if sobriety has degrees, because now, for instance, I am not completely sober, but more sober than I have been, so if it has this kind of degree, an ascending staircase, then there is no absolute sobriety where I could feel totally secure; this staircase has no topmost step, because each new level is a new illusion.

Lying, on my back, on the bed; room; opposite me the

white wall, the balcony door with the reflections in its glass panes. Her head on my breast. As if this, too, were a degree of sobriety, a station from which, when glancing back, it seems that what had happened had not really happened. As if our laughter, that unstoppable laughter, and those folk motifs were only strange products of my imagination; while we are lying here motionless, she with her head on my breast, cradling my leg with her thighs. She stirs. It would be nice to decide what belongs to the imagination and what to reality. As if she were waking from a long dream. "My hand went to sleep," I hear her wakening voice, coming from a dream, from a long distance. "I want to shove my hand under your back because it's gone to sleep completely," I hear her voice. So then this is reality and everything that's happened until now is only imagination. We've fallen asleep. It was a dream. I rise a little, her hand slips under my back. She's squeezing me. I squeeze her to myself. But it's no use. Although I can feel the squeeze, her body does not seem palpable. Squeeze as I may, it would need a stronger squeeze for me really to feel her, but no matter how much harder I squeeze, I'd need to squeeze her even harder. Because I cannot separate her body from mine, as if the two bodies had no independent borders of their own and weightlessly blend into each other. "Do you know where I am now?" I hear her voice, her calm voice, shuttling between dream and wakefulness but also as if issuing from me. "I am now in a meadow, it's a long and wide, a very long and very wide meadow where flowers are blooming, and it's as if I were a bug among the flowers; I can't see this, I only feel it, you know? I feel that I'm a bug." The meadow, the flowers, the bug with its shiny back, black beetle in sun-drenched spring meadow. "Boy, how terrific it is to be in the meadow, boy oh boy! If you could only feel how terrific it is to be a bug in this meadow!" I can see the bug climbing over tiny clumps of dirt among blades of grass. Her palm is feeling my back. "Boy, I have it made! Have I got it made, oh boy! Boy, your body is terrific! Your body is full of compressed air! I've never felt before that your body is full of compressed air!" Her palm is at my back, my ear is full of soft screaming, two tree trunks are lying in the meadow, but it's as if they weren't two tree trunks at all but, rather, I know, two thighs sprawling yet still like tree trunks; between the tree trunks a sled is sliding in the wintry meadow, gliding down a hillside, heading toward the two tree trunks or toward some-thing, maybe the thighs, and it slips inside; and is jerked back, it glides back up the hill, and then glides down again; up and down; dim fog in the wintry landscape

boy oh boy

I've got it

made

    oh boy,

        have I

           got it made

                soft screaming to the rhythm of the sled sliding up and down; but this is not even a sled! a drop-ping-and-rising elevator between two tree trunks or some-thing; it drops and rises, drops and rises between the two somethings; but it's as if this dropping-rising

dropping

and rising

is not even an elevator or anything like that, but it's me

in

the rhythm of her voice

oh my, your body is full of little bits of
compressed air! oh my, my body is full

oh boy

got it made

I've

got it made

I'm dropping and rising to the rhythm of her voice,
up and down; it's sliding, like the sled, in and out; when it's out,
it brings on the desire to penetrate; when it's in, the desire to
get out; up and down; rising and falling, like the elevator; but
now I know what I've seen, it was me, the symbol of my own
movements in the sled and the elevator; and that means I am
inside her body. But then I should be feeling it! In the rhythm
of my movements I hear her approaching voice

oh boy

I've got it

made

deepening-widening rhythm; and at the end of every
completed rhythmic cycle there is some hard obstacle, the kind
I must overcome in the next cycle; now I know, the reason I
withdraw is to penetrate her even deeper; each withdrawal is
the search for a more advantageous situation; but I am not even
moving forward, but upward; not deeper, but higher! with
every penetration into an opalescent space, and each withdrawal is a smooth sliding into the softly pulsing darkness;
screaming loud it pulses; the pulsing alteration of light and

darkness is alternately silent and screaming; but the light is not real light, for I can feel the hard obstacle, and I know that if this obstacle were not here, if I could position myself so that it wouldn't be, so that it would cease! then I could reach the real light! but where am I? if we are making love it's something I should feel! but I don't, being only between light and darkness, always bumping into that obstacle, I rise and I plunge in the rhythm of silence and screaming, and I bump into it again and again, this hard little obstacle at the border of light and darkness; what is this? I must know where I am!

where I am, in this unstoppable rhythm which is endless, no matter how it deepens, how it widens, it has no end, for the obstacle always thrusts me back! preventing me from reaching the end of my own rhythm,

I seem to see, as if my eyes were open, I seem to see the door of the balcony, the bed, covered with a white sheet, and her thighs as they clasp my knee. Yes. As if I were seeing all this in the evening light of a lamp. And now it's quiet. And there is no more screaming. We are not making love. Only my knee, it seems my knee has imitated the rhythm of lovemaking; my knee colliding with her pubic bone. But to know what it is I'm seeing is no help: I can feel the unstoppable rhythm, and it's as if the rhythm were the real thing, knowing and seeing it appear to be only a lie about reality; what I see I cannot feel, only the rhythm in that inner distance. Light and dark, light and the plunging back into darkness.

I open my eyes. They were open before, just a little while ago. When did I shut them? But it's as though they hadn't been open at all, as though I'd merely imagined they were open, as if I were seeing her for the first time,

she's lying on top of me as if she were asleep. If she is asleep, if she really is, and I'm not just imagining it, then everything up to now has been hallucination, a delusion. She is smiling in her sleep. Of course, a delusion; just feel this pervasive silence now; and how wonderful it is to look at her face, smiling in her sleep. But I can't

decide

whether I'm really seeing this or only imagining it. Just as I can't decide whether we had made love, or was it only that my knee imitated the act of lovemaking with her pubic bone, or that's also something I'm only imagining. I can't feel what I'm seeing! I'm trying to squeeze her hard to myself, but I can't at all feel I'm pressing her to myself because I can't feel my body. I only see it. Sensation is within me, the sight is without me, and the two do not meet. I must tell her this: I can see you, but I don't feel you, yet I do feel the rhythm, which I cannot see; for I can see you lying here, and that you are sleeping; still I feel as if our bodies were moving with the rhythm of lovemaking. I don't want it!

"Éva!"

Silence. It's as if now, in this silence, I could really see what I am seeing. Her head on my chest; she's asleep; she seems to be smiling in her sleep. But I have already seen this. And then, too, I thought I was seeing it, even though everything I believe to be real disappears, every time, everything does disappear. Under my head, I can feel it! a soft pillow. But I can't feel my body, though I can see it. But if I feel it, if at least I can separate the pillow from my head, then there must be something, after all, that I can feel.

                    "Éva!"

                              "Yes, dear. Yes. Yes, dear."

                                             In a hot shell, locked into the chain of

                                   repetition,

                                        yes, yes, dear

                                                  yes

                                                       how long has she been

                 saying this?

                              yes

                              yes

                                   dear

                                   then this must not be real, only the illusion of the real

                                   Yes, dear

                                        and in that case we can't get out of this, because she's plunged into it, too, and now my own dazed state is blending with hers

                                             yes yes

                                                  dear

                                                       yes, dear

                                                            Got

to

   wake up! Had enough!

                         yes

                              dear

                              "Éva!"

"Yes, dear!"

as if she were really saying it, and this weren't just a chainlike sequence of sounds, going on for how long now?

"Éva! Something strange is happening to us!"

"Yes, something strange."

As if, having risen from the depths, I were getting to the end of an upward spiral; from a remoteness that is not without me but within me: I'm safe, I have escaped; I can feel my own breathing; I breathe the air of a room, a room I can see. I can see her face, her eyes; her slightly bleary eyes made unclear by the exertions of her return to me; so she is struggling, too, struggling with the same thing. And I can see her skin's smooth tan, her long flaxen hair; and I know that I am here

"Yes.

Something strange."

I'd like to relate what has happened. What has happened cannot be told. As if it were not an independent occurrence but something identical with me, and the only way I could tell it perfectly would be to repeat it perfectly. Or maybe I could tell it if I could separate what has happened from what I think has happened, but only have imagined

"Éva!"

"Yes, dear."

"Something strange has happened to us."

as if somebody

were saying this for me, in my own familiar-from-somewhere voice; and as if this somebody, who is myself, had already said this before; but she is listening to me, leaning over me with such rapt attention! her attention an absolute certainty that everything I now hear or say is heard for the very first time; and if this is so, if I now have arrived at last in the concrete reality of the spoken word, of touching, breathing, and seeing, then everything I have until now believed to be reality, which has so terrified me with its real unreality,

has been

imagination.

Imagination, nothing else. And then it seems that even between the words I manage to say out loud I plunge back into this real daze, and it seems that this daze stretches time into infinity between two words; and in this stretching, expanding time, in the time of this daze, every kind of time is equally present. Present tense. Including the past and the future. Yes. I'm thinking again, though I wanted to say something, and if I'm thinking again, that means I got mixed up in that undefinable time stretching to eternity which I have just now formulated, so I could tear myself out of this time and return to the time which I've up to now believed to be reality, but this is impossible, because it is precisely with thoughts, by thinking this now, that I prevent my return, the chance to hold on to what I'd like to believe to be reality.

"Éva!"

"Yes, dear."

"Something strange is happening to us."

"Yes. Something strange."

"Now! Right now I'd like to get out of it. I'd like to tell you about it. To formulate it for you. Can you hear what I'm saying? Are you here? Am I only imagining you're here? are you in it?"

"Yes. I think I'm in it. Very much so. But I can listen. I'm listening to you. Do you hear me? I'm here."

Her, yes, I can always hold on to her. Not to my own thoughts or to my own imagination, not that. I'm thinking again. That's also a thought, that I'm thinking. I should stop it. That, too, is a thought.

No!

Yes.

The room. Now I'm alert. The brain is working ceaselessly. Alert at last. But objects are now closer, now farther away. I shouldn't be staring at them too long. They're moving. Her head on my chest. I can feel its weight. I feel that we are two separate entities whose contact I am allowed to feel; must be careful that these separate entities don't slip into each other again. As if she were smiling in her sleep. Her arm around me, she's here, her sunshine-colored thighs clasping my knee; I can feel the hardness of the pubic bone against my knee. That's what I wanted to say! But I mustn't wake her up! Is she really asleep? Didn't she just say something, I seem to have heard her voice, she did say something, but what? when? In the meantime, I must have sunk back down, and she must have fallen asleep. Good, it's all right like this, very good. The balcony door. Coming closer. The wall, white, coming closer, and everything gets bleached out, white, I can't see it anymore. When I look at something, it fills me up completely, I get filled out with it, it dominates me. No, I mustn't sink back. But what should I do, where can I escape to, when every second makes something happen? Could I outwit the whole thing if I closed my eyes?

It's growing dim.

As if I were lying not on the bed but in the middle of this increasing dimness, though I know I'm lying on the bed; still, I feel as if I were lying within myself, despite the fact that I can feel her palm on my back, her weight in the weight of my own body, the hard little barrier of her pubic bone on my knee. No. This I mustn't feel. I must invent something new before I sink again. Must invent something every second, and then I wouldn't be falling.

"Oh, you've got some body!"

I hear her voice coming out of her sleep, and I can see her voice, as it fills with brightness the dark space that is me

with the hard barrier of her body on my knee in a widening-narrowing rhythm

I am plunging

deeper

I am rising

I just wanted to ask if you said, did you or did you not say just now, or at any time, that

I've got it made

                            your body is full of little bits of com-
pressed air
                I like it
                    I've got it made!
                                    rising into opalescence,
                                          hov-
ering
      plummeting
                      into the softly pulsating
                                    darkness,
                                        boy oh boy, I
feel good
            where
                  am I? what's this? we're making love. No! no, it's
the same thing! but it's of no use that I know that this is the
same real disappointment which I have felt before. What good
is it, to feel it, and what's the point of feeling the very opposite
of what I know. Repetition. Everything is repeated. If everything is so unavoidably repeated, then I am in it once again,
which means that just a little while ago I didn't really get out of
it. Only now am I beginning to, really. But if this time I really
am getting out of it, that means that
                                  I feel it, I am rising, blend-
ing into the opalescent light with ease, and rising ever higher,
and I have never been to such heights, I know, in this ever-
expanding height where the end of infinity is always but a single movement ahead of me, and I keep rising and following it,
unstoppably
               falling
                      into the pulsating soft darkness, but then this

is a repetition, the repetition of hallucination, and if it is hallucination, then I did not get out of it; on the contrary, with
more and more certainty I am getting locked into this circle of
repetitions, a circle that has no exit; had only an entrance,
when? where? what circle? but it has no exit

"Éva!"

I hear, I can
hear the screaming, my own screaming above the pulsating soft
black space I hear my screaming, and I am hovering in an undefinable way

"Yes, dear!"

this, too, we have heard already! every-
thing is repeated and there is nothing new; if there was something new, and not this unceasing repetition, then I could get
hold of something, then I could tear myself out of this

"Some-
thing strange has happened to us."

I hear it, the words said in
my own voice, not as if I were saying them, but as if this voice
was simply something that had been heard before

"Yes. Some-
thing strange."

still, it is as if I were hearing it for the first time,
though I know it's not the first time, yet it feels that I'm hearing it for the first time; and if I'm hearing it for the first time,
then it's all right, then it's only inside me that time got all
mixed up; and if I'm hearing it for the first time, if this sentence
is identical with the one she said just a little while ago, but I'm
hearing it for the first time, because inside me, between two
words, all of time passes as it stretches into infinity, including all

its repetitions; if she is saying it now, if I'm hearing it for the first time, then imagination is

what until now I have believed to be reality, and reality is what until now I have believed to be imagination, and then I'm all right, because all I have to do is separate the two. I'm thinking again. I shouldn't be. But no matter what I believe, neither in reality nor in imagination am I able to feel myself. I rise, as if penetrating her body, upward and forward. I must feel

"I must feel!"

"What must you feel, dear?"

I must cheer myself up, I must not go under

"I must feel that I exist!"

"Do you feel sick? Unwell?"

what's she asking? unwell? what does that mean, unwell, unwell? unwell

"Are you unwell, dear?"

Something has been already repeated like this! Remember! This, too, is only a word that got here from who knows where! Remember! Who is saying this inside me? Remember! Remember what? Remember! Oh! I can't, I cannot remember because I don't know what I'd have to remember, I only know that if, again, I don't know what I should know, that means that again, once more, I wound up back here, without having found the exit.

Darkness that has neither height nor depth, a place where I am not, though I know that I should be. "I must feel!"

I hear the screaming; the screaming that is not coming into me but receding above me, out of me

"What must you feel, dear?"

I can see. I can see her face, too. She is looking. Looking at something. If she is above me, then she must be bending over me. If she is bending over me, then I must be lying here in bed. The place where I lay down, on my back. Then the pillow must be under my head.

"Don't you feel well? Are you unwell, dear?"

I can see the soft movements of the mouth, I can hear what I see, and what I see and hear are wrapped around me as a palpable body, though it's not palpable, it's only something I see and hear

"I should be doing something, I must feel!"

"Are you unwell? Don't you feel well, dear?"

unwell? from her voice, from the look in her eyes I can feel that something has happened to me, and whatever it is, it makes her worry. But I don't know why, after all I feel very good.

"Are you feeling bad, dear?"

"No. I don't feel bad, only a little while ago I lost myself, and I lost you because I lost myself."

It's good to hear that I'm talking. It would be good to

continue. Right now I exist, because I can see you; your hand is coming closer, and so is your skin, I can see the small bumps and hills of your palm over my skin; that's right, your palm makes me feel my own face, I've got a face, and I have to tell you that, because if I talk, and talk very fast, then I am, I exist, and then I'll no longer have the feeling that I don't exist even though I should.

"Can't you feel it? Can you hear what I'm saying? Your hands. Your feet. Can you feel your hands, your feet?"

how does she know that this is what she should be asking? the words, how funny! the uttered words describe, make palpable these hands and feet; her words make tangible what is mine

"Yes. I can feel them."

but I'd go on feeling them only if she kept saying out loud the words that signify my hands and feet. I haven't awakened completely. But if I did not feel my hands and my feet, if I couldn't feel myself, then it's possible that this, too, my being here, is nothing but hallucination. But didn't I just now—when exactly?—decide that this is reality, what up to now I thought to be illusion, and illusion is what I had thought to be reality before; and if I turn things around like that, then everything is all right. If I can't feel myself, then this is an illusion. "Are you thirsty, dear?" no, I'm not thirsty. "I must feel!" the tongue is groping its way, touching something, teeth; mouth! This is my mouth. "Shall I get you some water?" Now I can see her clearly. Her face, the room; as if she had asked something. Yes, this is the room. There is the door with glass panes, it opens into the foyer. This is the room where I am. This, at least, is for sure. These are immobile objects. Furniture. "Can you hear what I'm saying? Shall I get you some water?" she noticed that I was thirsty, my mouth is parched, how does she know I'm thirsty?

"I'll get some! I will get it myself! I must feel that I can bring myself a glass of water!"

I'm on my way. There is the door, it opens into the foyer, I have to open it. As if I were flying, disembodied, above the bed, I feel nothing under my feet; I only see the room swaying because of my movement; the very negative of my own momentum. I am standing on the rug and looking back at the bed, where I had been lying before. Naked body lolling on the bed, on the white sheet, in the yellowish light of the wall lamp. Brown female body, her white breasts adorned with even browner nipples; her loose, long, flaxen hair spread over the pillow. She is looking at me. But it's as if she didn't see me, her look passing through my head, observing something that is behind me, but what?

I look back.

The closed door of the foyer.

I look back.

The rug in front of the balcony's open door. As if her gaze urged me on in a way that has to do with the doors. I don't know why I'm standing here, why? That is where I was lying, yes; then I somehow wound up here, but I am no less uncertain standing here than I was lying down over there. Water. Yes, the water. Now the furniture and the light are in motion; it's as if charging out from the midst of furniture and lights a dark tunnel were running alongside me, silent and elusive; I'm flying. I can feel it, just slightly above the floor. A click. In the dim light I see a hand on the switch, my own hand, and a sink; the sink is bright, water is dripping from the faucet. I can see a drinking glass approaching the faucet. This hand, my hand, is grasping the glass, and from the faucet water is dripping. This is the bathroom. But if this is the bathroom, how did I get here? And if this glass is in my hand, when and where did I pick it up? If I am really standing here in this bathroom with the glass in my hand, and I'm not only imagining it, because I'm thirsty, as I do in my dreams when I'm thirsty, and if imagination is not reality, then it seems there are times that are beyond my control. Periods of time that occur outside my consciousness. On the other hand, if I turned on the faucet now and poured water into the glass, then this same time would turn into the kind of time I'm familiar with, because it would be me who filled it with movements. If I don't let time run away without me, I feel that I exist. My hand is getting close to the faucet, I can't feel it, but I see that my hand turns the knob and water runs out. I can't hear it, though I know I should hear the sound of running water, but I can see it. And if I am standing here in the bathroom, then the mirror is here, too, here above the sink, and in the mirror I can check, I can see myself. Face in the mirror. Pale, with matted hair. Black, deep wrinkles. Without the slightest doubt, it is my face, so very familiar, yet there is something dubious about it, as if it weren't even my face, because, search as I may, I can't see the eyes; only the grooves and wrinkles, the various features of the face are twisting and moving about, but I can't find the eyes that are looking for themselves; but I mustn't look too long, for then I'd sink, even though right now I am actually doing something, I am here in the bathroom to drink some water? I can see it: the face is fleeing the mirror so I won't see it. But the glass is not even half full, is this how fast I've been thinking? The water is gushing into the full glass, spilling out all over the rim, bubbling, running down my hand. I can see the water pouring down my hand, but I can't feel it. I have to get back to her. She's lying on the bed. To drink. I raise the glass to my mouth, I can feel the glass touching my lips, I can feel my mouth and hear the gulping, I can hear the path of the water, only I cannot feel its substance and taste. As if I were ill. She bends over me, she is making me drink as if I were ill. I can hear the swallowing sounds of the throat, but I cannot feel that what I'm drinking is some sort of substance, I only know it is water. Over the rim of the glass I can see the room I am in. I don't want any more water. The hand and the glass disappear. From under my head, I can feel, her hand slips out. My head falls on the pillow. The glass clinks. She's put it down. This clinking sounds realistic in this real silence. Here I lie. There is the open door of the balcony, the bookcase with its books, the white wall. The door to the foyer. Drinking glass on the side table. If the glass clinked on the side table, then I wasn't in the bathroom, I didn't see myself in the mirror. "Are you thirsty, dear?" My tongue seems to have swollen up, it can barely turn in the hollow of the mouth, feeling its way along the edges of the teeth. "Are you thirsty, dear?" "Yes. I am thirsty." "Shall I get you some water?" "Yes, please." Then she must have gone for water. The door to the foyer is open. It's dark in there. She appears in the dark, drinking glass in her hand, with her foot she kicks the foyer door shut and is coming toward me, her brown, naked body is increasing in size, she is coming toward me with the glass; the water is sparkling in the glass, as are the brown nipples in the white of her breasts. She sits down at the edge of the bed, slips her hand under my head, I can feel the back of my head, I can feel it, I've been lying on the pillow until now, now she is lifting my head and is making me drink, as if I were ill; her breasts are very close to me; as if I were ill, I swallow the water in small gulps, but I cannot taste it, it does not quench my thirst; her breasts, I seem to be wanting her breasts; the water cools only the swollen tongue, I don't want it anymore, I won't swallow any more. The hand and the glass disappear, I hear the clinking of the glass. On the night table, most likely it clinked on the night table. But if this is a real clinking, if I really see the room, if she has really brought me the water, then I wasn't in the bathroom, then I only imagined that I was and that I saw my face in the mirror.

"Éva!"

"Yes, dear!"

"Éva! I want to know now. Now I really want to know. Have I been out to the bathroom? Just now, was I out in the bathroom?"

As if she had been waiting for this question.

"Yes. You were out in the bathroom. You went to the bathroom to feel if you could do something. You were in the bathroom."

All right, then, that's good; good that she is here, and that I was in the bathroom, that she is leaning over me, because then I might even find her hand somewhere.

"Éva!"

"Yes, dear!"

"I'd really like to know, did you bring me some water?"

"Yes, I did."

Then I wasn't in the bathroom. Then I only imagined that I was, and I only imagined that I asked her about it, and also imagined that she answered me yes, you were in the bathroom. Then everything is all right: all this I am merely imagining. I'd like to find her hand. Ridiculous. As if I were ill, as if once before, while down with some illness, I had looked for a hand like that, and that hand is clasped around my own hand, and yet it isn't a hand but some dense, thick, heavy, living mass that swells, expands, flows into me, becomes indistinguishable from me, even though I know that all I am doing is holding her hand; I know I should be feeling that I'm holding her hand, but what I feel is that I am lying inside a gigantic, warm, slowly closing palm, I am weight-less, and in this feeling I cannot separate what is me and mine from what is her and hers; she might as well be lying inside me or I inside her, in the color of the skin, in the live and breath-ing flesh. It's good here, inside these two bodies, without boundaries. My senses, it seems, have once again parted com-pany with my consciousness. But luckily my consciousness is functioning well. I know I am here on the bed, only I don't know what I should know so that my consciousness could contradict my senses; and if my consciousness once again doesn't know what it should know, then perhaps it isn't functioning so well, after all; it is possible that it is precisely consciousness, thought independent of the senses, that is deceiving me; for if I don't know that what I feel is something I really feel or merely imagine that I do, then I cannot possibly know whether she is here, with me, really, or I merely imagine that she is. She is here. I am holding her hand, only her hand has grown impossibly large in my senses. But even if she is here and I am holding her hand, it is possible that she is feeling something entirely different, and what she feels of me is just as uncontrollable and uncertain as what I feel of her. I mustn't be thinking. Thinking separates me from sensuality and prevents me from feeling. I should draw her even closer to myself so she would feel exactly what I'm feeling and I would feel what she feels. Now is the time we should make love! if it were possible; if I could be master of my body. But if I pressed her harder to myself, and even if we made love, I'd know even less whether either of us existed or not. The closer she gets to me, the more I lose her, and just as she recedes I lose her for sure; for there is always this Me, always Me, and because of this ubiquitous Me I cannot feel and cannot know what I am or what She is in reality. I cannot feel it because I am thinking, even now. I feel nothing, though I know that everything exists, but I feel nothing, and that makes it possible that nothing exists, and that's the reason I cannot know anything with certainty. Nothing. I have already found, I always do, some kind of handle. Must find some reliable point. There is none right now. That I could grasp, get hold of. All reliable points are unreliable from a different point of view.

"Thir-
sty? Are you thirsty, dear?"

I hear her voice. I must have been licking my lips again, they've gone completely dry; but she has already asked me this question, too—when? Pay attention to time!

I can see, I can make out at least the open door of the balcony. Now I should get up and step out on the balcony so that I might see something, something other than the open door of the balcony. It seems as if I'm getting up, walking, but the door of the balcony is not coming closer. Though the time, this much time, should have been plenty for it; I am walking toward the door of the balcony, with this much time passing I should have reached it, isn't it only a few steps away? I can't find the steps I'm taking, even though I am taking them, one after the other, forward, but I cannot see my feet thrusting forward. There is no time. There are no objects, these are not real things! This is all imagination! That, at least, is certain. Now, about my logic; the very least I know of my logic is that it is functioning all right, it's in good shape; to every yes it has a no, and to every no it says yes; this is real. Only I haven't had the strength until now to admit and accept this reality; right now I have been torn asunder, into two completely congruent, logical parts: every-thing I know and feel is identical with what I do not know and feel; there is knowing beyond not-knowing, and not-knowing beyond knowing; and there is no end to it all. Noth-ing lies under something, and something under nothing. And still! I should feel, I should know that this balcony door is really nonexistent? Does it really exist? I've got to jump out!

The

bed is sagging, but I'm already on the rug, it slips under me. I bump into the railing, I lose my balance, that's the point I've been looking for! to swing across and then down down!

Thud.

Collision. Have I fallen down already? She is flailing her arms in the evening light of lamps, sawing the air, jumping after me, groping, wanting to yank me to herself, but I regain my balance, the room around me is silent, I am standing in the middle of the room, her face is coming closer because she is jumping, throwing herself after me, and there's some dread in her face, and I can feel that I am running away from her, but she seizes, yanks me to herself, our bodies clash, two kinds of flesh bang together. Stop! Why should I?

Silence.

I shove her away. Backward, she crashes into the table; her weight and the force of her momentum send the table sliding out of the picture, it disappears

the rug in front of the open balcony door. Empty. Waiting. I know I slipped on the rug, but the rug is empty, waiting for me in front of the balcony door, and if only I jumped on the rug, two more steps, I could jump out, across the railing of the balcony, and down down

the table is not slipping any farther; she is holding on to the table and starts for me

gets up from the bed; she is coming, coming toward me, with calm, long steps, and she is smiling

the two bodies, coming from op-

4 6

posite directions, meet on the rug and suddenly blend into one, and now she is coming toward me; she is coming, smiling, but

I'm here in the middle of the room. In her arms. We are standing in the middle of the room, and what I could only see before, as if in a picture, while we were standing in the middle of the room, I can now feel: her skin on mine, my chest on her breast. I feel that I am here, and lower my head onto her shoulder, and I see the open balcony door, which just now I've seen to be the same from an entirely different perspective; and also the rug and the bed, and I feel as if I had just jumped from the bed to this spot, to the middle of the room, where I am standing with her, in her arms; but this is not where I wanted to be, yet I am here, why? And my head is not even on her shoulder, because I can see her face, she is smiling; calmly, beautifully she smiles, as if nothing had happened.

"Éva!"

"Yes, dear. I'm here. Can you see me? Feel me?"

"Now I do, but I'm afraid; I feel you always for just a few seconds; always for only a few seconds do I feel you are really here, and I always lose the feeling. I don't want to, I don't want to lose you!"

this is ridiculous, ridiculously moving. I am moved, I manage to move myself, this is my voice, but it can't be real if it is so ridiculously moving, it is ridiculous that I so insist on her being here and that I feel so vulnerable; but she's pressing me to herself, I can feel it, which means I can feel, after all! very hard she presses me to herself, and me too, I am pressing her tight, too; the harder I squeeze, the harder she squeezes me; the hug grows weaker, the more I press her to myself the weaker I feel her hug to be

                                                   "Dear. Can you feel me now?"

                           feel only her voice, but I cannot see her, I cannot feel her body, even though I know we are standing here, hugging each other, in the middle of the room, I know it, if I am not imagining it

                                   "I want to feel you! I want to feel you! Something strange has happened to us! Again, again I feel that I am drifting away from her. And I feel, I know, that she is drawing near again. And I know that I shouldn't say this at all, but perhaps if I do it quickly, if I try to say everything real quick, maybe then! Can you hear what I'm saying? Hold me tight! Oh, I can't feel you anymore! Tight, hold me tight, just until I manage to tell you that the reason I jumped over here a little while ago is that otherwise I would have jumped out the window. The balcony door is open, and without wanting to I wasn't even thinking of anything like this, but if I hadn't jumped over here, I would have jumped out the window!"

                                                   "No. You will not jump out the window, dear. Do you hear me? You will not jump out the window, because I will not allow you to do that. Do you understand? Can you hear what I am saying?"

                                   "Yes. Now I know that I won't jump out the window, but please understand that I feel, again I feel that a long line is approaching, which I can see, and which I have to cross or something. I don't want to, but I always seem to have a contrary will inside me, and it wants me to jump. Now I know, I can feel, that I'm here, here with you; maybe it will pass, but until now I didn't know, not exactly, what was happening, or rather, whether what was taking place was in fact truly happening, d'y'understand?"

"Nothing has happened."

"Nothing?"

"No. Nothing has happened. You were simply lying on the bed and now you leaped over here like a billy goat! Nothing else has happened!"

"Nothing else has happened?"

"No. Nothing else."

"Éva!"

"Yes, dear."

"And in the bathroom? Have I been, in the meantime, in the bathroom, to get some water?"

"No. Nothing has happened. You haven't been to the bathroom. You were simply lying on the bed and now leaped over here like a billy goat! Nothing else happened!"

"Éva!"

"Yes, dear."

"And what about the water? Did you bring me some water?"

"No. I did not bring you any water."

No. It's all right, then. If I haven't

been to the bathroom, and she didn't bring me any water, then really nothing has happened except that I lay on the bed, and whatever else happened was something that took place only in my head, and now it's all over. And what if this is a hallucination? If it is all over now, and now all this is reality, and everything until now has been nothing but imagination, then how come I cannot see her, why can't I feel her? I am standing again in this black space. Or maybe I've lost her again, but only for a second? And all I have to do is open my eyes because, while I was thinking, and again I was thinking, while

I was thinking

the

sight unfolds: hugging each other, we are standing in the middle of the room. The room, again the room. Her head is on my shoulder, but I can't feel it. The bed, where we had been lying. The open door of the balcony with the rug in front of it. Evening lights in the room. Because outside it's dark. Night. That's why the light is on in here, above the bed. Then this light and this darkness are identical with that evening when we went to bed? Yes. I remember: it started with a soft humming and a heavy hovering, and now I have come back, have wound up back here, and once again can see what is visible. In the meantime, some time has gone by, but only within me, and in reality not that much time, because it's still the same: evening, with its unchanged lights, and nothing has happened, though I believed something was happening. I believed so many things! In the motionless non-happening: I believed everything from laughter to death. I must laugh, I am getting inflated with the suffocating spasm of laughter that had dragged me down once before; but now it seems that I have to laugh though I don't want to, I seem to be laughing at what happened, which in fact was but the appearance of happening, and still, how strongly she yanked me to herself! tragedy, death! while in reality nothing happened! how empty and ridiculous are these lofty concepts when we see only their shadows; while I was marching toward my own death there was a motionless room, right here, and I was in it, here, on the bed, also motionless. And if this is so—and I do feel it is, I really do, because I can squeeze her body with my arms, my skin can feel her skin, my belly, if I pay attention to it, can feel the curve of her belly; my chest feels her breasts, I can feel her head on my shoulder, the familiar fragrance of her hair; fragrance—and if I can feel all this, then this is the reality I've been struggling for so hard, and all along it has been in my hands. Here it is, I have regained what I actually hadn't lost. I have to laugh at myself, the one who deceived and fooled himself. But I'm trying to suppress this inner laughter which threatens to overwhelm everything: it should not break through the surface, I must not laugh, because if I do everything might start all over again, everything would be repeated; but why am I so afraid of repetition when I know everything that was really wasn't, I only believed it was! My fear makes me even more ridiculous; how ridiculous it is to fear something that doesn't exist. Is there anything to stop me from laughing freely? And if I still don't dare let myself go, that means I still believe imagination to be reality, I still fear something that does not exist! Though it used to. And now, now I know exactly what it used to be: I can hear, I can hear the scream again, and on my knee I can feel the barrier of the pubic bone. But there was no lovemaking—that I merely imagined: the lively imagination of my knee! I know everything, precisely, but I'd like to see her face, to make my knowledge even more precise: my palm slides up her arm, I'm making it slide, my palm lifts her head, the head rises from my shoulder so I can see it. I see the face. The shiny reflection of the lamp on the dome of her high, clear forehead. The light of the lamp within her blue eyes. Her slightly chapped lips as she runs her tongue along them. Her head tips to the side, she smiles as one just waking. This is the smile. That overly lovely smile. Coming from and reaching into infinity. I have to push away the body clinging to my body so I won't have to see this smile from so close, I have to create some distance: this is a real smile, not the one that lured me into the time of imagination. I know, this is a real smile, yes, still it is identical with the one that has lured me into laughter, into the infinity of repetitions. I am afraid. I can't believe her smile, it makes me feel uncertain. I can see her. I see her face, her neck, her shoulder, as much of the room as fits into my field of vision, but I'm afraid that this smile, right at the center of my view, is no longer a real smile, no matter how much these real-seeming dimensions appear to validate it! a smile in the space of my imagination. I'd like to believe in what I'm seeing! But do I really see what I see, or merely imagine that I do? I need something! Something is missing so terribly!

"Éva!"

"Yes, dear."

in the silence of the unfolding occurrence, the familiar stranger responds with her own voice; it is as if I were hearing this sort of sound, the human voice, for the first time, as if only now I realized for the first time that in the real world, which I have been looking for and whose totality I could not feel except gradually, in this world each image has an accompanying sound, that is, not only is there a picture—either visible and tangible, or in the form of thoughts about it—but there is also a sound! the image makes a sound, and perhaps that is the highest degree of experiencing reality! there is sound, which I used to know, and which I lost and then got back again.

"Éva!

And what about that, that thing really did happen, didn't it? I'd like to tell you. Now I'd like to hear your voice! Just a while ago, when we were lying there, you did clasp my knee with your thighs, didn't you?"

the body of my own voice; voice is the body become audible; yes, this is no smile from the realm of imagination, even though she is smiling as if she hadn't heard me

why doesn't she answer? her smile is swimming toward me, as if it had nothing to do with the face from which it had detached itself

"As if my knee! Did you feel it? As if I had made love to you with the thrusts of my knee! Did you feel it? As if my knee had embraced you! Did you feel it?"

out of the smile a voice emanates, radiating along her softly moving delicate lips

"No. I did not feel it. No."

"As if we had been making love! You did not feel it?"

"No. I didn't. This, too. This, too, is probably something you only imagined!"

What? This, too, is probably something I only

imagine. What? Why does she say that? How could she possibly know what I imagine? She can't, because what I imagine is inside, and she is outside, if she exists at all. She was here, just a while ago, but where? My own thoughts are replying to my own thoughts. Her I imagine only as one of my selves. If it were otherwise, then she'd be standing here, right in front of me, but she isn't here, there is nothing here, only nothing is here, I'm once again inside the repetition of nothing, at a place where Something holds out the hope of letting me catch it but, when I do, reveals its true self to me: as Nothing, which I believed to be Something. And if this Nothing is here, then I'm unable to decide where I am now. It's possible that I'm lying on the bed, but it's just as possible that I am standing over there or am still on the bed or may have jumped out the window and that's why I feel no ground under my feet, nothing, in this darkness. No, that can't be. I'm thinking. And if I'm thinking, then it can be determined where I am. If I follow the thought through. Let's try thinking logically. Only you can't, it's ridiculous, but you can't think logically, because you are not in possession of the tools needed to make logical connections between things. I'm ridiculous, I want to define myself with what I cannot define myself with. I could define myself only if I had one point, one single solitary point I could feel to be real, from which, having planted my feet firmly on it, I could look back to determine time and space; if I knew where I am and knew the sequence of events that are or are not occurring, if I could be certain about anything, I would tie myself to that certainty, that one unreachable certainty, adjusting to it everything I have lived through or imagined up to this moment, and at that point I could break out of the circle. Which probably does not exist. Which I find myself inside of, nevertheless. Where I keep trying to catch up with myself, but always find only myself, which is why I keep slipping through my own fingers. But this circle had to have an entrance! And if there was an entrance, there has to be an exit as well. The exit also leads to reality, which I cannot find. And what if we reversed the train of thought? What if we said: reality is not *that*, not what I've thought it to be up to now, but *this*. It would be all the same. If *this* is reality, then why am I obsessed with looking for *that*? Obsession is driven by will. And will is nothing but one's power deceiving itself. But it's useless to think about this; it's no use calling *this* reality, while what I'm looking for is *that*. Thinking is not to be blamed for self-deception, for thinking is capable only of reproducing things, it trails after the process. It seems that a more powerful force is acting upon me, rendering me unable to do anything for or against my will. And the only reason I can even think about this force is that this very force is acting upon me. No. This, too, is a false track. One shouldn't think. Must return to the entrance. Which we may call reality. Yes. There. We sat down at the table. We smoked the first one there, and then,

then,

then is a time definition answering to when? and *there* is a place definition answering to where? One question for every word! But it's impossible like that! If every word is questionable, then I can't get to the end of it! Table. At the table. But where is the table? Let us think about the table. Antique. Table. A square table. A square antique table. Table!

But I cannot see it, I can only add some concepts to the concept of table, concepts I have of a table I cannot see because I don't know where I am, if only I could know where I am, if I could determine the direction in which I should look, if I could wait for the time when I could

see

but it is precisely this point which I have lost, one from which any direction might have been determined: I have lost the entrance, which may still be called reality, and that is the reason I cannot find the exit. Logical. But for how long? Although with my logic I could return to the entrance, my logic cannot replace my senses, I cannot see with my logic; I am being controlled by a force stronger than I thought, but I cannot contemplate this force because I can only feel it. That's all that's left. This blackness, this black silence in which my logic is racing darkly along a circular, prescribed trajectory, always returning to verify itself. Always returning to the same ungraspable point: this is the sole graspable point of my logic. And that is also its flaw. What should be determined is not in which situation, when, and where I have been, but in which situation, when, and where I am. The idea is not to relate one to another, because using the circular reasoning of the past I cannot determine the present. How lucidly my mind is working! Measuring, enjoying its own suffering. But for how long? At the moment, it's functioning. Let's start with that! With what we've got. So then, something of me is functioning, even though it's only a fragment of myself. That means that in some form I do exist. This, however, is nothing but the flexible self-justification of functioning. My logic is logically justifying its own logic, which, without the senses, is illogical. I know: it is repeating itself. How to continue? A force of unknown origin is urging me to think about it. Now let's start with that. It would be obtuse not to think about it just because I am unfamiliar with it. Let's start with that. I should be thinking. If my thinking could, like this, justify itself, independently of vital sensations, without needing the external world for its self-justification, then it is imaginable, provided that I remain consistent in my thinking, that I am no longer what I used to be, that I have become a fragment of my former self, which used to be whole, and only in my logic am I condemned by that unknown force to justify my existence. Condemned: this is too mystical a concept, but I must make use of it since I do not know this force. If, then, I exist only as a fragment of my former, whole self, but this fragment now seems to be whole, that means I simultaneously am and am not, somewhere between my two potential human capacities. Where? Where my story is stripped down to its bare essentials: between existence and nonexistence. That's where I am conceptually. Visually: in black logical silence with the noise of lackluster thoughts. In other words, death. It's not that, yet. Yet it is, already. But where, and how? How could I check, to be sure that it is death? When, how could I have got so close to it? I didn't jump out; on the contrary, thanks to that unknown force, I've been prevented from jumping. And still I got this close? All I can know is that I am in between two of my human capacities. But just what these two capacities are I cannot know. I cannot know what this force, which is moving me, has done with my physical existence. Because I once again, since when? cannot feel or see anything, I am merely this mad galloping of thoughts. Which is to say that if I still have a physical existence, it has sunk back into insensateness. Into the force field that anticipates not only my thoughts but also my sensations, which I am trying to think about. Trying to think, but I see no pictures. There is a difference. Now and here it's no longer pictures that are happening to me; physical existence is only the surface of existence: the external world no longer appears to me, not even in the form of pictures. Thought is but a stripped-down, bare picture. These bare pictures are the only things I can actually feel separating themselves from me; my external world now consists of what is still identical with me: my logic. That is all that's left before nonexistence. The self-justifying rearguard action of physical existence. The anxiety of I-do-not-exist-though-I-should. Death. Or the sensation of death. I can't decide. To decide just what this is—premonition of death, sensation of death, or death itself—I should feel or see the physical existence which, for how long now? I haven't felt; that is, I'd need the external world in which I could feel myself. This sequence of thoughts is also a terminal point, returning me to the beginning, to repetition, to self-justification; I am in a logical system: in the same place. Thoughts are repeating themselves, just as the pictures repeated themselves. Now I no longer have to do anything. Letting go. Giving myself over because struggling would have been in vain. And even this state has ceased to be an *is*, this too has become a *was*. Revealing its own hollowness. If I lose my contact with the external world, if the pictures cease, then thinking remains the rear guard of existence. But left to itself my thinking does not know, cannot remember, does not relate to, and cannot feel what it is supposed to explain and what may be called the external world; it knows only these words, "external world," and these words meant something in the world with which it has parted company; thus, left to itself, the readiness to think finds no topic for thought: it hovers about, ruminating on some leftovers of logical generalizations. Which is still reality. Still! Let's forget it. It has revealed its true self. A mechanical skeleton. The last stop. But if this last stop is real, if I could at least remember, if I could strap myself to my memories, then it would be precisely at this last stop that I'd find the point I've been looking for! then I could think through the whole thing, backward, and then I might manage to get back. To where? Every statement brings on a question. Where to? This, this too must be remembered! I can't. Remember what? Remember what words mean. The external world, remember only the external world! What is that? The external world. Something outside me, something that is away from here, not here. Something else. Outside. Outside me, in the past, they were there, outside me, in the past. When? Outside. What? Some things. What sort of things? Objects. For example, objects. But that's also just a word! Try another way. Something! Needed! I am a person. Persons. Other persons. Who? Me! And who else? Objects. The most simple objects! Something! Words. But what is that? These words, which mean something I cannot remember. Cannot. Yes. Exactly! I cannot, the reason I cannot remember is that the pictures have ceased! if they'd appear along with the words, then I could remember. And they are all here, within me. Who? Where? I should remember somebody! Somebody, who! No, I can't see it, I can't see anybody, I don't remember anybody. I must see. They're not inside me, it seems that there is nothing and nobody inside me, I am completely empty, for only I am inside me, and then I have returned again

I

but I am not here either, because *I* is also nothing but a leftover word, which I only think about, a swollen nothing using this word as its appellation; nothing groping for something, within its swollen self, to prove its own existence. Then I know everything. It's all over. At last. Not true! For real knowledge this is either too much or too little. This is self-deception. Self-revelation. My logic isn't truthful either. How could it be truthful if it isn't real! I have entered a system, and I know only what has happened within this system, which is true, but how would I know whether it is real or not? The truths of the imagination. This I remember. Here, in this space, I know about everything. We smoked. Maybe too large a dose. I know that, too, that it may have been too large a dose. Okay. While we were smoking, it was still reality. That's when it started, then. The entrance to the circle is sexuality. My sexuality, which she does not feel, which does not reach her. It started here. Either she's lying when she says it doesn't reach her, because she wants to drag me even further into the circle, for good, so I wouldn't find the exit, she wants to keep me here, for herself, because she wants to gobble me up, for good. Or she doesn't feel it. She couldn't, because all this movement has taken place only inside me, with no external indications at all. But if the movement took place only inside me, if the pictures, the images of internal movement, are not real, then the self-justification of my thinking is also false, yes, false, insisting on proving itself so vehemently only to keep me here, not to let me break out. And if not only the images are false, but my logic as well, then I must be incapable of determining not only where I am but also what I think about this. Grasping at nothing, to do something with it. But there is nothing one can do with nothing, for it doesn't exist, and yet it has surrounded me. Leave it. Break out of it! If that force will allow, if it would, if it would sweep me along, then I could leave it, sometime, but when? and then it will end

will pop up, rising from the darkness, and in the distance, still far away, that line is still very far; it's coming closer, or I am getting closer, and past that line it's not so dark; there; rather a glimmering grayness; the line; there it is, approaching, or maybe I am approaching the line; it's the line that separates the blackness from the glimmering grayness, and I'm approaching so fast, it's unbearable; I need air! but still it's good, because I can see, the line is there, the one I have to cross, I can see it, it's really close now, I can see it! I can see, it's not the line that's coming closer, I am rushing toward it, weightlessly, I can see, I can feel already, as if anticipating while still rushing, the happiness of crashing across it: from darkness into glimmering grayness! faster, faster

I can see it, the darkness is approaching! why? why the darkness when the gray

the door the balcony stone railing dark behind the gray approaching, what is this?

where?

if it is approaching, then I

am running,

why
am I running toward it
when the glimmering was coming
closer

why am I running? I wasn't running! the carpet, that carpet! obstacle, what is this? no, I did not want to, I don't want to
jump out, the line! must flee! is that all this line means? but what
is this here? to flee so as not to see, not to! why not, if I don't
want to? if I don't know what it is I don't want, or where I'm
running to, then it's possible that fleeing, if I am fleeing, is taking
me closer, which I don't want! I don't want to jump out! hand,
arm, this body is flooding me with the color of skin! in the light
of the lamp: this is she; but how did I get here? I must flee from
here! I can see, I can feel, I am jumping up and down, flailing
my arms, lashing out, whipping the air all around me, without
knowing why or how I got here, where am I? why am I jumping around? got to flee, escape! there! to the wall! I can see her,
I don't know why she is grabbing at things, is she here? snapping
at things and jumping after me, but she shouldn't catch me!
why doesn't she let me go? but why am I fleeing, and where
to? when I don't want to be doing what I'm doing?
"Éva!"
"Yes, dear! Yes, yes! What? Tell me!"
Is she receding, or am I?
from the balcony this is pretty far, yes, this is a wall, all right,
then it would be nice to get into the wall, it would keep me, if
I rolled up into a ball, she shouldn't come after me! can't you
see I'm fleeing! this is not it! sure, there's no balcony here, the
balcony is over there!

6 2

"Éva! How much time's gone by?"

"When, when, how much time's gone by when?"

why is she yelling? precisely, I was in it again, and now precisely, this question must be formulated very precisely, but it's no use! precision is only a matter of degrees!

"How much, how much time's gone by? How much time's gone by since I've been standing on this spot?"

"Where?"

of course, the question, the precision! I wasn't standing here, I was standing over there!

"Éva, how much time has gone by, how much time's gone by while I was standing there?"

why is she afraid of me?

"None. No time at all!"

"How much time's gone by?"

"I don't know. I don't know, dear."

"But what time is it?"

wherever she is looking, the place she is looking at, yes, that's where the chest of drawers is: this is the room, the chest of drawers is there, she is looking at the time shown on the clock

"Half past twelve."

I can also see the clock on top

of the chest of drawers, among books, there is the clock, yes, it shows half past twelve, because the small hand is between the twelve and the one, these are numbers, and the big hand is on the six, shouldn't be thinking, but how could I see the clock since I'm standing not there but over here, and still I see the clock from close up, but then how long have I been standing here?

"Since I've been standing here, Éva, please, you see, I know your name, since I've been standing here, and not there, since I've been standing here, how much time has gone by?"

"Oh!

My! Well, none! No time at all since then, I just told you, I've told you that you jumped over here just now!"

"But there, how long did I stand over there?"

"Oh boy, where 'there'? You've been standing here, and you're still standing here! Dear, please believe me, you've been standing here!"

"Where?"

it's really as if I were standing there and not here where I've been standing?

"Do you understand? Can you hear, do you understand what I'm saying? None at all, since then, no time at all, you've just jumped over here!"

"Éva, no! That's impossible. Then I didn't manage to get out of it, after all, or you're mistaken, because I have been standing here for a very long time,

and where? I don't know. Impossible, for a very very long time.
I don't know. Oh boy, impossible!"

                              no,

                                   I don't know, am I
standing there? or here? when was I standing there for a long
time, or here? I should explain this: if you looked at the clock!
the clock is time! time is the only certainty! interesting, this re-
spondent is not asking questions now, but helping me! who is
this, within me? But how could I see the clock from so close
up if I am standing there and not here. It is half past twelve.
That is the *now*. This is the only certain *is*. As of now.

Everything that is now gone may be considered the past. This hand is my hand. I can see, I can feel my legs and my thighs, but why do they keep rising, now this one, now the other, as if I were running? why are my hands flopping around? I am jumping up and down. There is nothing wrong, I'm just jumping. This naked body is me. It's only my head I cannot see, but of course I can't, because the eyes, with which I see, are located in the head; I can see the body, the carpet, the floor. These here, for example, are objects. And there is the balcony, too. If I had jumped off the balcony, I would have crashed into the street. Street. I can recall even that word! "Street." If I decided to leave here and started running out there, I should probably tell her to come on, let's get out of here, let's run on the street so I won't have to keep seeing the same things over and over again; but if I started out and ran

"Are you thirsty?"

I can feel my tongue,

my tongue on my lips; maybe that's what thirst is. She is standing in front of me. Smiling. Does that mean that I'm standing here again, where I stood before, and not there? or maybe I haven't been jumping around, and only imagined I have? Not much time could have gone by.

"Do you want me to get you some water? All right? I'll bring you some water."

I can see the face. Lovely. Well-proportioned. Trying to smile, though I can see that this face doesn't feel like smiling, and she mentions the water, she brings me the water only to help me, I can see in her face that she's afraid of me, wants to help, but it's not quite clear why she should be afraid of me and why she should help me. Interesting. If all this shows on her face, then she too must be full of thoughts, just like me, she too is completely filled out, no gaps in her at all. That means that she is a real being, and I am not only imagining her.

"I'll bring you some water, all right? Are you afraid of being left alone, dear?"

Water. She is bringing water. If she is bringing me water, then there must be something visible on my face which I cannot see. Something that gave her the idea that she had to help me because I am not in my normal state. She is bringing water. Something, then something is wrong with me after all. Most likely, otherwise why would I be standing here, naked, in the middle of the room? Night. Yes, it's night outside. I am ill, and I am standing here. Where has she disappeared to? She's gone to get water. By the time she gets back I should clarify just what it is that's wrong with me. I shouldn't be standing here like this, so motionless. I can feel the step I'm taking, I am headed for the table, but by the time I get to it I can no longer feel I've taken a step, only that I am here. I can see it: I stamp my foot against the floor so I can feel my sole! But I can't. Once again I look and see that I stamp my foot. It should hurt, but it doesn't. Quickly I raise my arms, sawing the air, I can see the swinging of the arms, but by the time they reach their uppermost position I have the urge to start running. Constantly to invent new movements, so I won't get lost. The objects move about me, as if they were running. Judging by the pace of the sight around me, I am the one who is running. But I can no longer feel it. I squat down. This I can feel. I jump up. Action always precedes thought. When did they close, who closed the door? I've got to check the time. I am standing, facing the closed door of the balcony. Is there someone else in the room who could have closed it? I look around. Now she is not here, now I could jump out. But why should I, if I don't want to? Or maybe it's not that action precedes thought but rather that action stems so quickly from a previous action that my thinking cannot follow it? I am here. But how did I get here? I don't know. I have lost my memory, a link from the chain of actions. But when? I can see the swinging arms, the knees bending so I could squat; the legs straightening for the jump, which means that this is what I'm doing, alternately squatting and jumping, even though I am standing right here, stock-still. I can see the swinging of the arms, I can feel it, I squat down, jump up, even though the sight before me does not move, here I am, standing motionless, and the objects are also motionless, while if I were really moving, not only imagining it, then everything I see should be moving, too. I run around the room once, I can feel it, and I am standing here, motionless, I can see it. Simultaneously I feel and see my own motionlessness and movement, as if there were a third person observing these two persons who are me, though in fact I am all three. No. Only this third one is me, who, between these other two, is watching those who are me. The one jumping up, squatting, running, squatting, leapfrogging. Circular swinging of arms. But I can't feel it. Time is too long between two movements. By the time I get to the next movement I lose the sensation of the previous one. The first other, who is constantly moving about, is driven by some compulsion, just as the second is compelled somehow to be motionless. But I cannot know the nature of the compulsion because this is not me, I can only see it. This one is moving about so as to feel what he cannot feel while standing still; so he has gone mad, because no matter what he does, he has lost contact with realistic movements that can be felt as well. He is getting lost, lost in the cracks between movements; he's got too much time between two movements. Faster, he's got to be moving faster, but even between two fast movements there is a pause. One movement could catch up with the next only if it were identical with it. But if I execute identical movements, then I lose all sensations, because everything is merely repeated, and in the eternal sameness of repetition I can't find myself, because I am not identical with what is being repeated. I should run away, somewhere, maybe blend into the wall. And I should adjust myself to the time. I should be able to see the clock, but if I don't know where I am, then I can't possibly know where the clock is.

seems that I've been standing here, only my eyes have been
closed, because I was thinking again; the objects moved because
I was thinking, but now the clock is here. Time. The big hand
on the six, the small hand between the twelve and the one.
That means it's half past twelve. It is? How could what *was* turn
into *is*? It stopped at half past twelve. But if it stopped it
wouldn't be ticking. I can hear it, it's ticking. Half past one. If
it's not the clock that stopped, it's the time that stopped. After
all, the clock is not time, it is only a means to show what time
it is, how much time has elapsed compared to another point in
time. But one should know the previous point in time. And
that is something the clock does not show, even though it is
ticking. We've already had half past twelve. Ticking. It's half past
twelve now. Then something must have happened to time. It
has stopped. It doesn't show what it should, which would have
been the only certain reference for me, a kind of handle on
time. I surely thought so. This, too, has revealed itself to be
what it really is. Time is standing still; only in my imagination
does it move on. The very last morsel of reality has also proved
to be nothing but imagination. But this act of proving is also
nothing but imagination. Repetition. The repetition of the fact
that my logic has already corroborated: I have reached a terminal point. Most likely this is the moment, this half past twelve,
this time, when my being has ceased and I no longer exist, only
until now I have believed that I should. Physical existence's last
attempt to hold on by grasping at thoughts. Time has lost its
validity. The clock is nothing more than the symbol of invali-
dated time. I've got to get going. I should help myself toward

my own cessation, since that is what is wanted of me. Let's concentrate. Now I can see the clock, which means that if I keep turning I will see the room, too, where the balcony door is open, and then I can start out, because I can be sure that is where I want to go

"Here is the water, dear."

she is standing here, in front of me, as if she had been standing here always, as if she were identical to her former self, with a glass in her hand, water in the glass

"What happened?"

"Nothing."

she is handing me the water, but she is receding, because I am backing away, fleeing toward the wall, running away from her, who isn't, who doesn't exist, but with the illusion of her existence she always manages to hold me back at the last minute

"What happened?"

and I really didn't mean to shout, only I feel such a restlessness within me

"No. Nothing has happened. You just ran around a little bit. Nothing else has happened. But don't be afraid. Nothing else. And now I understand what is happening to you, dear. It's probably something that is going on inside you. But don't be afraid! It'll pass in a minute. And I'm right here with you. Can you see me? I'm here, and I am staying by your side, and it will pass in a minute. Drink."

she is

coming closer, reaching out, handing me the water that I should drink

"Éva!"

"Yes, dear."

"And what about the water, did you bring me water?"

"Can't you see, I did bring you water. Drink."

I'm looking at her. That means she's really here, and then I can drink the water, the water isn't turning into imagination. I probably am thirsty. Then I should believe her. Then so far, up to this moment, nothing has happened. Then I can accept the water. I'm reaching for it, her hand is on my shoulder, and over the rim of the glass I can see her smiling face; her face is trying, but this is no smile, only an effort to calm me down. She's suffering. I must have done something to make her suffer. I shouldn't do that. I must be careful not to make her suffer, because she's so good to me, she stops me from doing it, she's patient with me even though it's nighttime and I've been jumping around for no good reason except that something is happening to me. I can hear the gulps pass my throat, but I taste nothing, feel no texture. It's frightening; after all, something that cannot happen might be happening. Quickly I take the glass away from my lips and hand it to her. She takes it, puts it on the table; it's as if this, too, had actually happened. Glass knocking on wood. If that knocking is also something that really happened, then

"Éva!"

"Yes, dear, what is it?"

"How much time's gone by?"

"Since when, how much time has gone by since when?"

"Since I've been standing here!"

"Nothing, really, no time's gone by!"

"Éva, that's impossible! Éva! Please tell me, I don't want to ask you, but please be kind enough to tell me, and don't be angry, but please tell me what time it is."

"Half past twelve."

"Éva! Exactly!"

"Half past twelve!"

it's as if I'm not hearing what I should be hearing: half past twelve. Is that possible? Now I remember: it was half past twelve a little while ago, too, and it was half past twelve once more before that. But since then some time's gone by. Or I just imagined it. But imagination has its time, too; imagination outside time is an impossibility! Or time has stopped. Or it's not imagination but me who is outside time. I just got proof that this supposition is correct, because she is telling me, so I must know, that my time has stopped. If it's half past twelve now, and it was half past twelve before, that means that it will always be half past twelve. Or she is lying.

"Half past twelve! Do you understand? Half past twelve! Do you understand, dear? It's now half past twelve. Half past twelve. That's what time it is. Not more, not less. Half past twelve. It's half past twelve, darling!"

she's whispering; but her face! If she weren't lying, her eyes wouldn't be narrowing so sneeringly! she wouldn't be whispering, wouldn't be hissing with such hatred, wouldn't be showing herself to be so beautiful even now, if she weren't lying. Her beauty, too, is nothing but an illusion, an allurement, so that I believe her lies. If she could make me believe that it's half past twelve, then I'd also have to believe that time has stopped, and then I couldn't possibly control anything, then I'd have to stay here forever. With her. She figured this out, down to the last detail, well in advance. She has lured me into these circles of illusion which, she figured, should also make me accept as fact that time has stopped. But she forgot to take into consideration that I can still think. Only I can't. So she's won. It makes no difference whether or not I think, or what I think: the fact is, it's half past twelve. To think properly about this fact I would need one other, a single other point in time so that I could compare the two. What I have is two identical points in time. It was half past twelve, and it is half past twelve. And what if a whole day has gone by between them? if it's no longer today but tomorrow? A full twenty-four-hour period, a whole day gone by! This I could check only if I could wait. Five minutes. I can't wait, because time is not moving. Half past twelve is what was and has been, and it is half past twelve right now. One can wait only for something that is yet to come. The unknown, the anticipated. One can't wait for what has already come to pass. Waiting has ceased.

The clock! Maybe!

It shows half past twelve. And there is the balcony door. Open. I can feel this force within me, how it has been quietly observing things! but I am no longer allowed to feel it, because it now takes off and runs toward the open door, and I can see that I'm running toward the open door, but the door is not coming closer, it is receding, and I feel I bumped into something. I wasn't driven to the door but to the wall, over here. I'd like to touch the wall with my hands, but I can't reach it, no matter how much I flail and swing my arms; and some tension, maybe because I can't feel the wall, is making me kick and jump. Here we are, standing in the middle of the room, even though it seems I'm over there, by the wall, having fled there so I wouldn't jump out the window. Yet I am not there but here. And she is here, too, though until now I haven't seen her, where has she been? She's been here all along, only I haven't seen her. I can feel that my hands are not moving, my legs neither. It's quiet. And more and more certainly I see that she is here. I've got to take advantage of this time.

"Éva, I feel I've gone mad. I can't get out of it! Right now I think I'm in my right mind, for the moment. Now everything is in sharp focus. Now everything is here, but that also frightens me. I'm scared! Do you understand? Scared! Everything disappears. I want to tell you quickly, while I'm still here, Éva, something should be done. I've gone mad. I can't get out of these fast-moving pictures or thoughts, and I never know where I am because time is not moving."

"Visions? You see visions?"

"I don't know. It's not that I see pictures of things that don't exist; what I mean is, that's exactly what I don't know. It seems I see only what there is, but I'm not sure there is anything. And everything there is has become faster, but time is standing still. I can't separate things. I don't even know, though just a while ago I did know! and now I don't even know whether you are really here or I merely imagine that you are. Because everything has become dark, and I can't see you, I can only hear my own voice and know that I'm talking, but I cannot know whether I'm talking to you or just to myself. Please don't be angry; if you are here and can still hear what I'm saying, please, don't be cross, though you always seem to be saying things that confuse me. As if you want to deceive me. Please don't be cross with me."

"You know where we are?"

"I do. I know this room. I can see it very clearly again. But I don't know, no matter how hard I try to remember, I don't know what's outside this room. I know I should know, but I don't know what it is that I should know. Only words come into my memory. And everything is being repeated; and it's as if I had already said this before, too. And there is this force within me that keeps wanting to hurl me over there, you know? Out the window! but something stops me. My other me. But I don't know which me is me.

Help me!

It feels as if I'm having a conversation with myself, and I am imagining you only because I won't know for sure whether I'm talking to myself or to you. Help me! I'll never be able to get out of this room again. You can't possibly want that. Where are you? I can't feel you. You see, once again I can't feel you and

77

I can't see you, because you didn't help me. I am not completely crazy, yet. I can still think a little. This room exists, only I can't see it; and I know that I exist, too, only I can't feel myself, and you, too, you exist, too, which has led me to conclude that something outside you must also exist. Only I don't remember what. Now I do! See, it's just occurred to me. You see, I know, you see I also know, because I remembered, that there is a telephone. On the night table. And if there is a telephone, we can call an ambulance! Call an ambulance! And they'll come and take me away, because we can use the telephone. And they'll do something for me, because I can't stand it anymore, don't be cross, but I can't bear it. But what could they do for me? I've gone mad, what could they possibly do for me?"

"Dearest! Please listen to me! Can you hear what I'm saying? You're so pale again! Listen to me! Just concentrate on me! Do you hear me? I'm here. Dear! Everything's all right. It will pass. Everything will be all right. Do you hear what I'm saying? Everything will be all right! Understand? All right, all right. D'you hear, oh dearest, do you hear what I'm saying? d'you hear what I'm telling you? try to lie down! I'm all right, you've got nothing to worry about. I'm right here beside you. Do you hear what I'm saying?"

"I hear you. But that means I haven't been talking to you, only imagined it. Do you understand?"

"Everything is fine. Can you see me?"

"Yes."

it's as if now I'm truly

rising to the level of the scene that is taking place. The one that was here all along but I didn't know about it. The one that doesn't exist except in my imagination. We are standing where we have been standing. Between the table and the bed, under the chandelier. The light is on over the bed. So it's evening, nighttime. But if it's nighttime, then why are we standing here? Why is the bed empty? Something is wrong with me and that's the reason I won't let her sleep. Even though it's night, and tomorrow she has to go to work. So, I do remember something after all. Then I haven't gone completely bananas.

"Éva!"

"Yes, darling, talk to me!"

"Shouldn't we? Shouldn't we call an ambulance?"

this I've said before, or imagined before

"Ambulance? No! It will pass. Everything will be all right. Don't be afraid. You've had too much to smoke, is all. If I called an ambulance I'd have to tell them that you smoked. And then they'd lock us up, both you and me. In jail. And that wouldn't make any sense, would it? Do you get it?"

I seem to be rising even higher, out of some sort of depths where I've been, from where I had already seen that this room was here. But even now it seems as if I were not in the room I see. But where, then? A cell. If I'm able to imagine a jail cell, which belongs to the outside world, outside this room, then I am able to remember. So if we call the emergency people with the ambulance, they would take me to jail. That's the reason we shouldn't call. But if we don't call, and they won't take me to jail, then when would I get out of this room?

"Éva!"

"Yes, dear."

"Éva, I think I'm completely down, all sober. I know you're right. But I'd like to know."

"What, dear, what would you like to know?"

I'd like to know, but I'm afraid to ask, because you might give me the same answer! I can see my feet jumping up and down, that means I'm jumping; my hands would like to overcome my fear, I can see my hands lashing out at fear; forced movements; so I'd rather ask just so I won't have to deal with these forced

"What time is it?"

"Half past twelve."

she is not looking at the clock. But if she is not, how does she know? and it's no use looking at her face, because I can see in her face that she is not lying, she is certain she is telling the truth.

"Half past twelve. It's half past twelve, dear."

Then it's all right. At least one thing is for sure: I've gone crazy. Once again I'm in the black nothingness which I know and which seems to be my only real place. So, the way things are, I haven't seen anything, I haven't heard anything either, I merely imagined what had already happened, or could have happened until I reached this final point in time. I am still aware of this: I stepped into the circle that had an entrance but no exit. By doing that, however, only my own efforts took on permanent form. By doing that, I did not get out of myself, rather I fell back into myself. What had been there all along became permanent. As the result of my ambitions, desires, and lies. I've lost touch with the outside world because I was afraid, I've always been afraid of it. It has been too confusing, too impenetrable, and too complicated for me not to be afraid of it. I believed that if I simplified it, cut it down to my own size, I would understand it. The whole world within myself. It was a lie. The lie of someone running away. But that's what I wanted, without the outside world to be the outside world of my self, letting go of all possible handles. I lied to myself, claiming that whatever I didn't understand did not exist. And now the outside world has really disappeared. The will to live should urge me to reach out and grab for it, but my lies have carried me in the wrong direction and it's no use grabbing if there are no more handles to grab. This is the end result of my cowardice and malleability. I'm reduced to what I really am: a lying, fallible being, destined to die. This is what I am, this is all I can call my own. But this is no longer life. Life was a relationship that bound my unknown symbols to the unknown symbols of others. Therefore, everything I have seen here until now simply doesn't exist except as some kind of symbol within me. She also is just a symbol that exists within me, that of femininity, which I have tried to hold on to, because I felt it to be the very last handle, since the objects of my desires are not without but within me. Yet the outside world—which up to now I've believed to be reality, and which I wanted so much that I was willing to deceive myself—is beyond her, and beyond me as well. I can no longer get there. Because that is no longer me. I have become two completely congruent forms, which is the reason I cannot feel my other self. Or this one, the one I call myself. If there were a God, I should take comfort in this ultimate contradiction. And if I had found that comfort, if I could calm down, I wouldn't be engaged in constant repetitions, the force of recognition would cease swirling in its own sphere, which is me. Even now I must be moving about, making some compulsive movements, but I cannot see them or feel them. But if I cannot calm down, if there is no force to suppress this other force, then there is no God. Then I lied, and God is also one of my lies. Then only I exist, entrusted to the voluntary movements of my own force, in the endlessly repeated recognition of my own symbols. But if this is true, then there is a God, who is me, which is this force operating within me yet independent of me. It keeps my repetitions going for as long as I am alive. Which is to say that death can put an end to them.

The excitement of recognition is boring because, no matter how hard I try to get out of the circle, recognition can catch up only with itself. It must get past death, into that other system, so that it becomes cognizant of more than just its own reference points.

There is nothing left inside me that would put up a protest. I don't even want to wait for her. Here I stand, and am turning into what I will not be. Where? That's right, not there, not anymore. Not between the table and the bed; the table is now behind me, and I am standing before the chest of drawers, and I can check how much time's gone by. But why would I still be swayed by time's temptation? The small hand is between the twelve and the one, the big hand on the six. Half past twelve. At last something that corroborates not my but its own existence. But of course everything corroborates only itself; and it's not only time I'm incapable of knowing but space, too. If I am not standing where I stood before, and cannot remember whether I changed places as the result of an independent decision, that is to say a decision made of my own free will, then all this points to the independence of space. Space is throwing me around, just as time is clinging to its own power. But this is not necessarily true. It is possible that some sort of force exists outside my will, yes, maybe it's that certain force within me, and it moves me about in space, but with my own logic I cannot fathom the functioning of this force. As I once used to, in that life referred to as normal. Events used to occur without my willing them to, and only afterward could I think about them, and only if there were points of rest between occurrences. That's what we used to call life. At the moment it is these gaps in logic that make my madness so lifelike. Madness is life, too. It still is. Life without the possibility of lies, in the absolute power of the force.

Glimmering twilight beyond the horizon of the dark field. The line separating darkness not from light but from the space in which the possibility of light exists, however faintly; which is to say that the space beyond the line is a shade lighter than the field I'm in. It isn't coming closer, neither am I getting closer to it, even though I have seen it approach before.

I am standing here, and I shall stumble across the

line to be there. Yes. This is the demarcation line of death. A symbol. I probably wish for this stumble, because over there the compulsion to glance at things, to evaluate, compare, and think about things, will probably cease. Beyond that line either everything is logical, and then I won't have to suffer from the yawning gaps between the links of logic, or everything is completely illogical; but complete illogic, which at the moment is still impossible for me to imagine, has no gaps either.

I did see it. So I know where I have to go, where I am going without having to.

But I'm not getting any closer to it, and it isn't coming closer to me. Maybe it is waiting for a decision? In this madness full of gaps, where it is no use looking at myself, no use looking at or testing the outside world, I always get back to the same questions; this condition is simply intolerable. I tolerate it, I do, but it's unbearable. This tolerable unbearableness, if only it hadn't resembled so persistently what it left behind! what I had believed to be a normal, real life. But how could it not resemble it when it is part of it? only it throws life's gaps into an even sharper relief. It seems that one's ultimate conclusion of life may be that one strives for gaplessness. Death. What ultimate conclusion? This is the one true thought! One that nobody else can use, the thought no one can think along with me, because I cannot possibly convey it to anyone, and therefore it is perfectly superfluous even for me.

Why isn't it coming closer?

I can reach it only if I manage to return from madness. It seems it's not a superfluous thought. I must think, I am

forced to think by the same force that eventually, and merci-
fully, will deprive me of the ability to think. The unknown. The
gap. The mover. The gapless within the gap. Where I strive so
hard to be. But it seems that I'd manage to roll into that dimension of existence only if first I could return to where I
started from. Let us think. I am in a logical phase of madness.
In this condition I function only in my thinking. Which could
be called life, because it is the sensation of not only my mental
but also my physical functioning. The fallacy of the simultane-
ity of body and soul. My mind has managed to comprehend
the symbolic meaning of the line beyond which none of this
exists. But I can reach this line only if for a second, for a fraction of a second, I can regain my physical senses, and among the
real spatial elements of symbolism, I can realistically direct my
body toward the kind of point that might make come true
what my mind has comprehended. It is my body, which I know
but can't feel, that I must regain and force into accepting
what the mind comprehended as fulfillment; to terminate it.

No.
Something is off here. Two chains of logic linked together only
by the insertion of a gap!

Let us think. If I am so keenly aware
that there is a body, decision, and will, and further, that there is
a world outside me that can be comprehended by the senses, a
world I do not now feel—once again I don't but I used to, and
could possibly feel again—then I must not have got her so close
to death as I thought; this has been the work of imagination, of
the imagination of madness. The refuge of madness is the kind
of final refuge that verifies not the existence of death as a sub-
ject, to which I have fled, but on the contrary, the existence of

the verb, the fleeing itself. In other words, it doesn't mean that with the help of death I might be out of my madness but rather that I have sunk even deeper into the logic of my madness. I have wound up in the phase of madness in which everything that has been and is still within me—will, affection, and thought—is beginning to jell into a system, a system that fills out its own body, with no gaps, and has no need for the sensation of the body, for the system is itself the body turned into thought, into the matter of logic; that's why it doesn't need the outside world either—nor could it have any use for it. The outside world ceases because its relationships would be incomprehensible to the system, alien to the homogeneity of the system's logic. There is no death. It would be an easy way out, only there is no such thing. Death would be the hope of redemption, which in this way, twisted out of its original meaning, or perhaps turned back exactly into its original meaning, means immutability. But there is no death. Only what there is, is: racing repeatedly along this circular course, in my own unknowable space where experience is meaningless! always back to the same place and without the reassuring reference of time, without the hope of redemption. I cannot possibly know how long I will have to go on living in myself. The average life span of madmen is shorter than that of those who believe themselves to be sane. This life span is shorter because everything I feel and think, the empty forms of my systems, I feel and think them much faster than those who in so-called real space and time cannot feel these empty forms. My rate of burning is faster. Ten years. At least ten. But how could I have hopes in these ten years, how could I bear these ten years without the hope of time's passing? when my time is not moving forward, and I don't know how much of *their* time has passed! Becoming idiotic, unhinged, going nuts, yes, going nuts. The insane, after a while—again time, but I cannot know how much of it—but after some time the insane go nuts, become idiotic. Probably at the time when their ability to suffer ceases, when this speed, this unstoppable extreme rhythm that knows no rest, becomes unbearable in the infinity of motionless time. When the contradiction between the inside and the outside world is no longer tolerable, when the body, brain cells, and nerve tissues die off before their final death? when the spirit puts an end to itself, right inside the body, leaving behind an empty, vegetative shell. But when does that happen? In five years. But if it is half past twelve now, and not a single one of those minutes I had known in the past have passed, then when will the five years be up?

Yes.

Calm, rest, silence, which do not exist. There is only one solution. I have to kill myself.

However, if the space I am in now is not a real space, if I merely believe it to be so, there is no point in running toward the balcony door; it seems I keep bumping into this obstacle of death, because at the place where I think the door is, there is no door. There is a wall. And maybe it's not even the wall of the same room I think I'm in. Because I cannot use time to check whether I'm really at the same spot where I once was. I cannot know how much time has passed for these objects. What has passed is so long that it could be months or even years. I'm not here anymore, I'm somewhere else, only within me this room somehow got recorded as the last territory of my real self. I have been taken from this room. The ambulance. This word could have occurred to me only because some time ago the ambulance team did come and they took me away, but then this fact has reached me from a great distance, since, no matter what has happened around me, my mind is kept captive by this room; and somehow the word still reached my mind and later fitted itself into the structure of my mind's obsession. And then I told her to call an ambulance. Even though she hadn't been there for a long time, and she had called a long time before that, and they took me away, and still I imagine I'm talking to her, asking her to call an ambulance, because I wanted to get out of that room. Even though I wasn't there anymore. I'm not there anymore. My obsession: to keep seeing this room. I know I can't get out. The total confrontation of will and existence. Without a shadow of a doubt, this is what madness is. But how could I get free? I should run somewhere where I would not see the object of my obsession, this room! But how, where would I run if I haven't the vaguest where I am? I should run. But I cannot.

I can feel it, I'm running . . .

but what's the use of running if I keep seeing this room! Why am I running if running is no solution, only a compulsion, the compulsion of flight, which means madness. I'd like to escape madness! But how can I escape what I am? Think, I must think! Now! Think!

Yes. There are two possibilities. There is an outside world. I know that. I must concentrate on the outside world. To understand fully, clearly, unclouded by obsessions to perceive and feel what the outside world is. Or I shall kill myself. But how can I kill myself while it is a wall there and not the balcony door, which I believe to be there?

And it is closed. It was open a little while ago. Change in the system of repetitions. But the change occurs, and this, too, is merely a symbol, only to make the system appear even more lifelike to me, to bind me here even more strongly; to confuse my logic. The folder. On the radiator; my old watch on top of the folder. Time. I could take a look at it, but it would be of no use. This is also a symbol. The longing for freedom. This longing is awakening in me, awakened by the will to live, yet there is nothing I can do: I am doing things in my imagined room; if this was seen by the outside world, it would be considered nothing but compulsive movements. From the outside world all they can see is that now I am walking over to some spot, lifting up some object which for them does not exist, and taking a look at this thing, which for them simply isn't there, and I break into a smile; how dumb they are! they cannot see I'm moving over to my old watch to check the time

"Dear! Can you hear me? Dear! Talk to me! Say something, you hear?! Say something! Anything! When you speak it's a little better, I think. Talk. Say something! Do you hear? Try it, talk! What do you feel? What is so terrible? Talk! Do you hear? Talk!"

but something is happening; something is happening, which is not me, as if I were hearing some voice! some kind of voice! as if I had heard something that did not come from me but rather is coming toward me from the outside! Or is it me talking to myself?

"Talk, dear! Go on! Say something! Your hands, your feet, do you feel your hands, your feet? Do you?"

my hands, my

feet, yes; of course! my hands, my feet! I can feel them! I can feel my hands! My feet! Through her voice I could feel my hands and feet; then I've escaped, I am safe

"Do you feel them? Talk to me!"

that means that I haven't felt them until now, but her voice, her voice makes them conscious, makes my hands palpable, and my feet—but it would be useless to answer that I feel them when I don't, again I don't feel them

"Can you feel them? Tell me!"

I can't answer because I can see she is standing here, the symbol is standing right in front of me, but I can't feel my hands or feet, I can't. Yet I should reassure her, which means reassuring myself; to reassure; so that her face will not be so scared; if her face is this scared of me, if I am this scared of myself, then all this is not merely a symbol, after all; then maybe we do exist, and then I also have hands and feet, only I cannot feel them

"Yes. I can feel them."

"Oh, dear! Talk! Yes, always answer me! All right? Tell me, you should always tell me what you feel! All right? What do you feel? Are you afraid? Are you anxious?"

could this be fear itself? if this is what they call fear and anxiety, then I am definitely afraid and anxious. But she has already asked me this before! It seems to me that she has already. She isn't here, and neither am I. I fooled myself once again. These old questions and answers must keep coming back so that they can appear to be real points of reference in the logic of madness, provide some variety in the monotony of repetitions; their purpose is to refer to the logic of existence, which is believed to be real, where it was their fickleness that made occurrences so lifelike. These questions of reference are the products of my own playful consciousness, seductive invitations for me to make an effort to return to what I had wanted to accept as reality, but since that is impossible anyway, I should sink even deeper into madness. I should be frightened and anxious, that's what they want. But I'm not; and I won't be fooled, I have reached the point where I can very calmly engage my own obsessions in conversation; fear? ridiculous

"Dear! Do you hear me? I'm here! Can you see me? I'm here, next to you, oh, I can't be any closer to you than this! Can you see me? Can you feel me? Talk to me! Don't be afraid, it'll pass! Do you hear? It'll pass. You don't have to be afraid! Do you know where you are? Can you see? Try to remember! Do you hear?"

it's as if she is talking, as if I were trying to encourage myself speaking in her voice

"Try! You have to want to! D'you hear? Try to remember!"

"Remember what?"

there is a face here, the face that reminds me of the face that used to be hers, but maybe it's only the mouth of my own face opening up

"Something! Remember anything!"

"I can't. No matter how hard I'm trying, I can't remember. I could remember only if I knew where I was. Yes. Now I can feel, now I can see that you are here. Are you here? You are, aren't you? Help me! Help me, so I won't slide back! Éva!"

"What?"

"How much time's gone by?"

the face which is in front of me; the eyes in the face begin to move, rolling this way and that, as if looking for something

"I don't know. No time at all. Hardly any."

"But how much?"

"A minute. Maybe one minute."

"Since when? If a minute's gone by, then what time is it now?"

"Half past twelve. A minute after half past twelve."

it's all right, then; I'm safe; it did pass, a minute went by; it doesn't stand still

"Try talking to me! All right? Or should I talk to you?"

"No! Don't! 'Cause if you did, automatism would take over right away!"

she's scared of me because I'm talking nonsense, but how should I explain it to her?

"What automatism, dear?"

"I don't know. That's how I feel. Once something starts,

it immediately becomes independent of everything else; it becomes a process; but no matter what starts happening, I always wind up in the same place. Do you understand? I wind up at that line. If there isn't something new, some novelty in every fraction of every second, I immediately slide back into this circle, my own circle, I lose you and I return to that same place. Do you get it? I lose the belief that you are real, even though I know you are only an illusion."

"You know what you should do, dear? Try counting."

"Counting?"

"Yes. Do you remember the numbers?"

"Yes."

"Then try counting. All right?"

"Un, deux, trois, quatre, cinq, six, sept, huit, neuf, dix, onze, douze, treize." "Great! Go on!"

"Treize, quatorze, quinze, seize."

"Go on!"

time is hopping along with you, from number to number, you can count, number after number, but when would I get to the end of it if number after number after

no!

if it passes only when I keep counting, then I don't want it; I can't do that, I can't spend five years, or ten, or who knows how many, just counting; but why did I count in French? why not in Hungarian?

I don't

want to know! why don't you want to know, dear? remember! remember what? why not in Hungarian? why in French? why did you count time with French numbers? I don't know. Try to remember! I can't. I should remember something I couldn't possibly remember. But I'm pretty sure that there is some important reason why I did not count in Hungarian but started with French numbers. And this reason is hidden from me, dear. Because I can't remember. Remember! Remember what? Who is asking? Your instincts. It is the instincts that are trying to clarify themselves within me, dear. Hungarian instincts, or French ones? Whatever I am. But what is that? what am I? Somebody is always asking questions. I myself am asking questions, I am asking me, I am asking myself. But I have no answers. Neither in Hungarian nor in French. Time cannot be counted. While I was counting something in French, the counting did not even touch time, never; the numbers were either before or after time, but not one of them had anything to do with time. I can't figure out time by using numbers. Because I cannot stop. I cannot orient myself to a steady, reliable point. There is no rest. The force is driving only my logic, so that it would prove things that are superfluous even for me. I am walking, but not forward. The essential always reveals itself through the superfluous. I've had to live through it all until now, superfluously, just so I could get to where I am now. So that the force can prove to me that there is no such thing as forward; therefore, counting forward would be pointless. Forward is but a concept I simply have to give up. There is no forward or backward. The impossible proving itself impossible. A circle that provides no experience except its own emptiness. Why should I endure all this?

Why must I survive all the failures? Why must I, always in the same circle and sinking ever deeper, get to the same place again and again?

"You'll make it, dear. No problem. I'm here, with you! I'm here. You'll make it, dear! No problem."

It's good to hear. Though I should know she is seducing me. Her calmness, self-assurance, and trust are seducing me. She is seducing me with the hope of returning to the same place. A seductress of returns! She is prolonging, filling out the time of my suffering. But slowly I am steeling myself against her. I can no longer believe she is real. I know, this is the temptation of the life force, which is talking within me in its peculiar form just as death does with its own signs and signals. A dialogue. But it is precisely this dialogue that cannot be prolonged any further. The final result has been produced. And if I cannot terminate this final result, too, then I will have to go on. And wind up, again and again, at the same place. Minute after minute. Ridiculous! A ridiculous concept from the past. And she told me about that one minute just to give me some hope. The trump held by the will to live, against death. The illusion of that one minute was provided by the life force, against death. Or maybe she was the one who actually said it, but only to deceive me. It's all the same. I can feel it: time is standing still. And I cannot just keep marking time indefinitely. Ask her, check with her! No, I don't want to ask her anymore. Time is moving, passing, it is only your illusion that it has stopped! No, don't ask, disappointment could only deepen your madness! But if you asked her, she'd tell you what time it is!

"Éva!"

"Yes, dear."

"How much time's gone by?"

"Since when? None. No time at all!"

"But what time is it now?"

"Half past twelve. It's half past twelve, dear."

Yes. All right. I checked, I asked. It has to be brought to an end.

"My dear! Listen to me. Try to lie down. Go to bed. Sleep. Try to lie down."

No. I won't go on experimenting. I won't try anything anymore. Enough. No matter what I try, I come up with the same result. I've got to stop.

"You'll make it. Nothing special's happened."

If I cannot terminate myself, I should just pass quietly away, slip out of myself.

"Lie down. Sleep it off and it'll pass."

No! I don't want to lie down. I don't want to hear this damn voice anymore! Enough! I can't stand it anymore!

"And when you wake up, the world will be exactly the same as it was before!"

No. I don't want it to be like that! It will not be, for it doesn't exist, it just doesn't. Why must I be listening to these miserable voices of mine? Why are they talking to each other, tearing me apart, when all I want is to pass quietly away.

Schizophrenic psychosis.

Just what I needed, another definition! I don't want it! I don't want it! Let him out of himself! You are locked up! Can't you hear, you wretch? Let him get out of himself!

Within a white frame on a smooth dark surface dull spots and sharp fields of light. Outside—but it's impossible to see outside, it's night outside—reflected light and blurry spots spilling into one another in the glass of the balcony door. Because outside it's night. And the room is full of reflected light. Whatever was yelling and rumbling inside me a while ago is now receding, and as it pulls back into its own dimness, its place is being taken over by the silence of this room; a motionless sight. And I can feel the room taking its place within me, thus I return to myself, to what I was. Here I stand, and there is nothing extraordinary about that. Somewhere in the middle of the room. But not only do I see it, I also feel it with my skin that I am standing here, and there's nothing special about that. I can lift my hand a little, and I can actually feel that. I can lower my hand, and I can feel that, too. I can feel reality, which is still fragile, for I might lose it again, but it is here, nevertheless, beyond all doubt it is here in this room, and it has returned to me, too. I have to be careful, should not move around too much, so I won't lose it. The empty bed, the folds of the crumpled white sheet. The smooth diffusion and flashes of light along the edges of objects. This is also a system. Reality is a most extraordinary system in which one is imperceptibly passed on from perception to perception. If I am standing here, then I cannot be standing there. This is the law of reality. And while I was moving from here to there, the countless different parts of space would be passing me on as if from hand to hand, and I'd always wind up there. This is time.

"Lie down, dear. All right? You'll sleep it off, and it'll pass. And when you wake up, the world will be exactly the same as it was before."

It is already. If possible, it is even more the same, because I am glad that it is. And I am glad for this voice, hers, which blends so gently into the silence of this room and the silence of my thoughts. I turn my head to the side, and slowly, in exactly the same rhythm in which I turn my head, the image also turns. That means I can turn it, this is how it is in reality: if I can hear her voice, I can also look at her. And there she is, standing by the table. Yes, the table. Where she sat before. And all this is so natural and simple that she is not surprised at all. But her face is tired; fatigue is in her smile. How feeble and miserable I've been by myself. But she struggled, fought, wouldn't give up until she dragged me back here. And she got tired. I'd love to step closer to her, touch her. But she's fragile; I fear for this fragile, simple system of real feelings inside me. The gentle features of her face; the breasts on the squat, almost ungainly body; as if by magic, the breasts, which hardly ever stop quivering, with their dark areolae on white flesh, turn this large body into something so tender. But I can touch it! I am taking steps in her direction, and stepping means only one thing: taking a step toward her.

I don't think I have ever said this to you. I love you very much."

My confession is acknowledged between the palms of my hands; squeezed between my palms the smile is beginning to spread; my palms feel the warmth of her skin; the smile seems slowly, cleverly, to be freeing her face from its fatigue; but in fact it's the opposite that happens: the smile shows sharply how tired she is, my confession cannot revive her; it is a routine smile, a polite shield against my emotions. My, my, until I've reached love! It's been such a long road. No wonder: the drudgery has extinguished her love, the same love that revived me. How absurd. Two-way traffic on the same stretch of road. I wonder if she feels it. Can she feel at all how much I love her? In what sort of words, in what gestures could I couch my love? How could I pluck fatigue from her face? How can I make up for all the wrongs I've done her? How could I chase away her sadness caused by my indifference, motionlessness, and madness? Until now she's been fighting for me, now I have to fight for her. The human factors, two that are never equal. How familiar! But isn't this struggle for each other what we call love? Of course, that's only a word. Isn't it her struggle for me that I love in her? I've been fighting for her, too, and against myself, I suffered so that for one moment I could reach her, her, who is not me. But why is love like that, so tied to matter? Why can't love love itself—in her? Why can't I sense what she can,

without me,

just her! purely for herself.

No! Be careful! Thinking like that is what makes time stretch. What has happened is nothing but the long time of love. Struggle for me, for her. In retrospect: what a pleasant and fun time, what amusing adventures of self-deception. The time of love that has extinguished real time. The time that ceased, and fought against itself, so that it could revive love in me, love mortified, love degenerated into sexuality. This is how time is returned, time that was stolen by the time of love. It has been returned with love, which is identical with her nameable, real being.

How lovely! Here we stand. Night in a city. In similar barns similar animals spend the night. Rooms. People. But of what is happening in here, nobody can know anything. Of what is happening here with us, and what is so similar to what is happening to them who are so similar to us, nobody can know anything. The miracle of reality's infinite variations: here we are, the two of us.

"Are you tired? You're probably tired, dear. Try to sleep. I'll stay right here with you. All right? Nothing can go wrong. I'll sit by you or, if you want me to, I'll lie down next to you. Lie down. All right? Try to sleep, dear. Everything is all right."

No. She doesn't feel anything of the things I feel. But that's all right. Time is continuing. To sleep. To rest. Next to her. This, too, in the time of love. The bed. This means I have picked a point in space which I can reach.

She leans over me, her breasts touch my chest. If she is leaning over me I must be horizontal, not vertical. I must be lying down. On the bed. Yes, that is the point I've picked out in space, the one I reached. But when? The very movement of lying down, its rhythm, got lost somewhere in time. No matter. It seems that for a moment, while I was lying down, I slid back a little.

"Should I get you some water, dear? Aren't you thirsty? Lemonade? All right? Or water? You're not thirsty?"

still, I feel everything is simpler, I'm much more clear-headed than before. Lemonade. Lemon seeds at the bottom of a glass. She is bringing water. Just now I was getting inflated by some wave of sentimentality; right now I am simply lying here. No wonder: from my imagined horrors I've slipped into the image of redemption. Luckily, she hasn't taken it seriously. I must be careful, or go to sleep.

The church bell strikes, resounding sharply in my ear,

one strike,

pause,

and then the next strike.

It struck twice. No more. The whole apparatus is creaking and groaning, I can hear it. And then there is silence. That means it's the half hour. Half past something. Time doesn't let me sleep. Was this meant to be a signal? For me! Signaling that I am not making any progress, not moving forward, I only imagine it. But why am I thinking about this when I wanted to go to sleep? No matter. I must be careful not to turn back from this reality, and there will be no problems at all. That church bell was a signal of time, so that I should not go to sleep. That I should be continually aware of what there is and what is happening around me; I can't go to sleep; if I fell asleep I'd lose time. Here I lie, and because I continue to lie here, that means that time is passing. But how could I fully, consciously realize that?

Here I lie.

Here I lie.

But if I keep on lying here continuously, I cannot feel that I'm lying here, because that is nothing but another automatism, the automatism of lying here, it's all repetition, the repetition of lying here. Sameness. In one set of time I lie here exactly the same way as in the other, which means I have no way of knowing when it is one set of time and when it is the other. I've no way of knowing whether or not what now *is* isn't identical with what *was*.

I should look at the second hand. Is there a second hand on my watch? Yes, there is. That means I can remember. All I have to do is stretch out my arm, to the radiator; the second hand is on my watch, which is on top of the folder; but if I stretched out my arm, however carefully, that would be a movement, which means I wouldn't be lying here anymore. If I were not lying here, like this, without moving, then maybe the process would start again and I wouldn't know where I am, here or there? Movement would lead me into my own trap. Must be careful! Or am I already in the trap? The contradictions should be harmonized. Can't be done. To lie motionless, but in such a way that in every fraction of every second something new and different might happen. If every occurrence would move within me for only a specific period of time while I'm lying here; if every occurrence, in every second, would yield its place to the next one, then I'd never have to look at my watch; I'd be the motionless object, the clock, and movement would make time tick inside me; occurrence would use me to measure its own time—me, who'd be identical with the occurrence. While motionless, I could be the place of my own occurrences but also their measure as well as their object. Complete, gapless sameness: cessation of the contradistinction between inner and outer. Where there is no need for time! A new obsession. Its essence is the same: there's no point in trying to reach a state of motion or motionlessness; time can place itself inside me only in the motionlessness of my death, but for now I still exist, even though I'm lying here motionless; I still am, my thoughts are moving, and yet time is standing still as if I no longer existed. As if at half past twelve I had ceased to exist. But now I know: if I cannot induce my real death, I could get out of the system of my obsessions by grasping at those points of reality that refer not to sameness but to variability. Which is not the repetition of what has already occurred but the emergence from repetitions. I must be careful; I must find a point like that. So far I've taken good care of myself, now I must be really careful and find that point.

Water. Perhaps the water! She's gone out to bring me some water. Lemonade. I've already had lemonade. Water. But water isn't a new motif either; water is also a recurring motif of the system. Woman offers water to suffering man. A paradigm. Once or twice already she's gone out and come back with a glass in her hand, and gone out again to bring water. Repetition of the paradigm. If everything is repeated, then each phenomenon, image, and movement is an involuntary motif of the system. A motif that, in a schematic depiction, symbolizes something. She is a motif, and so am I. Our relationship is also a motif. She repeats set movements, while I keep running along the set circle of my logic. From the same point back to the same point, each along his or her circular course. The two circles can neither link up with each other nor, being circles, turn away from each other. Which symbolizes the fact that even if we cannot touch, we do need each other. I'm racing along my course, and just when I reach death, she reaches a certain movement along her course; with her movement she seduces me to seek life, to keep on moving. This appears to be real, because seemingly it isn't the same as, but rather a variation on, one of her old movements. The illusion of this newness jolts me out of the system of my repetitions. Movement is also a motif. Water is the motif of embracing and encouragement; which is to say, it is a motif that may appear in three different forms: as matter, as the idea of matter, or as an idea. But these motifs essentially symbolize nothing but the feminine struggle for the continuation of life. The possible variations of movement are infinite. Yet I'd be confused if I did not feel that all movements have the same essence. Movements are symbolic motifs. And the more I fight for the unambiguity of reality, the deeper I sink into the sense of symbolic ambiguity. Because I am thinking. Struggling in vain against my own thoughts. I am thinking, unable to accept or reject anything as final. Because my thinking is time itself. Cessation of thinking would terminate the motif of time in me, and my existence would cease as well. However, my existence is not allowed to cease, not allowed by her. Who in a certain sense is a personal, and in another sense an impersonal, motif in my system. When she appears in the personal form, she yanks me toward cessation, dissolution, getting free of life; that is to say, she symbolizes death. When she appears only as a motif, she is the obstacle placed in front of death, symbolizing life and love. And between these two extremes I keep running around my circular course.

Real and unreal, true and false—these are not two different, and therefore independent, systems. On the contrary. They are part of the grand system. After all, in these pairs one component exists only in its relation to the other. Only in the system of unreal relations can I see something else as real; and only while moving in the system of real relations can I consider something I see as unreal. When, therefore, I try to separate the real from the unreal, I am shackled by obsessions, delusions, and faulty logic; I don't know what to do with excessive knowledge. In fact, I can move around in only one chosen system of relations. To move in both at the same time is simply impossible. Somewhere between the two there is probably a stable point from which both systems may be viewed, but trusting in one's ability to find this point is but an illusion. If I move about in a single, chosen system of relations, then the motifs—movements and images reduced to their essence—take on a configuration that proves nothing but their existence. In the system I am moving in right now, everything proves one thing: time has stopped. And I am compelled to believe this proof, I am compelled to become the victim of my own system, until another system of relations would affect me so as to make me realize that not only my system of relations exists but other systems exist as well. Which is to say, not only I exist but she does, too. This realization has a powerful effect on me, like a new discovery, and for an instant it ejects me from myself; but to understand it fully I am forced again to rely on myself, that is to say, on my own system, which means that I continue on my own course again until I reach the very same place as before; and if I reach the very same place, the automatism of thinking once again drags in the appropriate final-conclusion motif: if there is no new place in space, in this case in the space of thought, then there is no new time, either; which is to say, if the current space is identical with the old space, then the current time may also be identical with the old time; time has stopped. There is no such thing as time. Of course I know that time hasn't stopped, it has only in my system, but this—a fact that seems unreal in the logic of the other system—I am compelled to accept as real because the system in which time moves forward I am unable to reach;

it takes this long to bring a glass of water?

It's the same with everything. Everything that I think might be proof of time's movement ultimately proves one thing: my time reaches into infinity and therefore is standing still.

And why is it dark in the room when only a little while ago it was light? Who turned off the lamp? Did she? when she left the room? She left me to myself on the pretext of going to get some water. But this fact is no cause for alarm. Proof: she has deceived me with her apparent presence. I am immovably bound to the real illusion that she is at my side. When she's by my side it's her presence, and when she isn't, it's her absence, that torments me. Torments, because I haven't been able to reconcile myself to the realization that illusion is also a reality, only the other side of reality. I might relax, if only I could fully comprehend what this means. Thought, if only as an experiment, might try to move about simultaneously in two different systems of relations. To compare the two opposing sides of reality. Let us think. The illusion that she is not here probably reflects the fact that while I believe myself to be in this room, standing in unmoving time, I am really somewhere else and have been for a long time. I am there, at a place where madmen are kept. But I cannot get free of the notion that I am here. I am *there* precisely because I haven't been able to shake the obsession that I am *here*. All right. Not here, but there. But where? I can see only this place, what's in front of me, here! If I could only tell them—yes, them, who surely exist and deal with madmen, with me, of course—if I could only tell them about this sharply drawn line of logic, one that keeps returning to itself! then they might get some insight into my system, into the logic of insanity; nor would they consider my movements compulsive movements, because they'd understand that when I stare at something, or jump up and down, these actions have very real, realistic significance; they'd know that I am not making compulsive movements but rather checking the time, or trying to jump off the balcony, or simply struggling to regain the sensation of my self. And that's exactly what makes me a madman, that's what distinguishes me from them; from them, who believe that time is moving forward

they have never asked themselves the question: forward, yes, but where to?

but that's exactly what distinguishes me from them: I am unable to permit insight into myself, because my system fills me solidly, gaplessly. Because I am my own obsession, my own fixed idea: the perfect, total identification.

The church bell strikes once. I am waiting for the next strike. There it goes. No more.

What I thought to be an external noise was in fact an inner one. A motif. I warn myself by using my watch. And no matter that I'm thinking, or that I feel new discoveries taking shape in my mind, it is still the same time, the very same time.

But why am I still waiting for something else to happen? Why can't I resign myself to viewing things in this set of time? Resign myself! Ridiculous, but it would be nice to know what they, those who have definitely made themselves believe that time moves forward, it would be nice to know what sort of time they believe to be theirs now that I have drifted away from them; and since I have, I don't know what they think. But there is no difference! What difference there is is the difference between the systems of relations. They are unaware of the time of the universe, of the grand system, just as I am unaware of their time.

Maybe it's nighttime.

If I'm not aware of the illusion of this beautiful woman by my side, that means that the outside world does not now want to affect me; which also means that if the outside world, which at the moment is the insane asylum, does influence me in any way, then this influence appears not in reality but in the form of this beautiful woman known to me from my past. They probably feed me, bathe me, keep my physical existence going, but if they do feed and bathe me—that is to say, they do affect me in some way—then I see not the real form of this effect but my own fixed idea, my obsession: this beautiful woman. But right now she is not making an appearance, right now I see only this dark room, the objective space of my obsession; this means they are leaving me alone, they believe I am asleep; yet my eyes are open, because I do see the room. It would be very nice if they left me alone for a very long time, because the woman's appearance would make the force go into action, and my affections would begin to function; they would make me gullible, which in turn would make me vulnerable; and then I wouldn't know what I know and what I don't know, and this irreconcilable state would lead me to death, to the real experience of the illusion of my own death, which I can neither induce nor endure. If they left me in peace, I could very calmly wait for my death. That's also what they're doing, waiting. But they also entertain themselves with a much richer system of motifs.

I have lost the sense of my existence, I only imagine that I am.

That is why I am unable to sense the existence of others.

I am pared down to the fundamental motifs.

That is why I cannot sense the rich system of motifs which they call life. That's why there is no reality, only symbols

My life is the

repetition of symbolic motifs: a permanent, complete inner sameness.

That's why there is no time.

But I know more than that. There is time. Birth and death. Motifs are born, motifs die. A certain variation of these nascent-and-dying motifs is called human being by the variation called the human variety. Humans: variations of the same gesture. Gesture: the rhythmically repeated movement of the force; exhalation, inhalation; birth and death. Rhythm is what man designates as time; rhythm is what is called birth and death. It is in the rhythm that one comes in contact with other variations of the gesture, also nascent-and-dying, since they are the motifs of the gesture, such as stones, trees, animals. This contact is called life. But the whole thing taken together: the rhythmic, varied repetition of the same thing.

I have lost contact with other variations of the gesture; getting to know them in this rhythm called life is both amusing and impossible. I feel only the gesture, the rhythm, the empty force in the empty form.

To those who feel only the differences in, and variabilities of, these nascent-and-dying motifs, this rhythm—yanked out of infinity simply by being named but, in fact, impossible to remove from infinity—might appear short; they say that the time of life is short; because the number of variations surrounding it is unfathomably infinite. Therefore, there is Many, to describe all the other motifs, compared to which theirs, the human variations, are Few. I do not feel the differences among the motifs, I know about them only because

I have taken part in the pursuit of trying to get to know them, but now I know that variability means not essential differences but in fact essential similarities. For me, then, the time that separates me from the end of the rhythm, from my death, for me this time seems long, because within me the gesture no longer sees or recognizes its other variations, only itself, the gesture.

If the variations are the unfathomably infinite motifs of the same gesture, with an identical essence, then how can we claim that time exists?

If I, as one variation of a gesture which in all its variations and motifs is essentially the same, am still capable of sensing and feeling other variations, able to make comparisons, then how can I claim that time doesn't exist?

I've gone nuts. Crazy, and lost in my own logic again. Again. Again the same motifs, the same reference points of logic.

I should give up the notion I have of real time and maybe then I could have some rest. To break away at last from the system I've been living in; their system. As it is, I am only struggling between the two systems. But again this feeling of irreconcilability, this I can't stand. I can't bear it. Then I am probably jumping up and down again, or making the kinds of movement they cannot understand. Please, kill me! Why don't they? Why are they letting me suffer like this, left to myself, all alone?

They are not planning to kill me. But in that case I have to think, and I can't stand that. I have to kill myself. This, too, is just a thought. The

thought of suicide being repeated. Motif. Symbol of life's in-
viability, of the inability to die. But it is only a thought. No,
I can't endure it. I've gone mad. But this is also something
I know! I know. I know this already, and why do I always have
to know the same thing?

All things considered, madness is noth-
ing but one's permanent irreconcilability with time. Irreconcilability with certainty, and also with uncertainty.

I know this, too.
I've known it before. Why do I have to know it anew, why
am I not progressing? I'm in it again. Back where I started
from.

God! This word. This word is not identical with what I've
thought it until now.

If only I could pray! Prayer is repetition.
With the automatism of repeating rehearsed words, prayer
makes you turn to yourself. The very place I want to run away
from! But then everything, everything that comes to my mind
is me, only me; it can make me turn only to myself, always and
only to the same place.

"Music! Would you like to listen to
some music, dear? Do you hear what I'm asking you? Do you?
Music? Jazz or Mozart? Do you hear me? Music! Dear, please
answer me, dear! Shall I put on some jazz or Mozart?"

"Mozart."
It is quiet.

As if sounds were approaching; they keep coming
closer, though I am not moving. But I can see the sounds as
they rumble noisily toward me from far away; sounds! sounds of

some kind! Several sounds, lots of different sounds, yet they are coming in a unified mass. And they are here already. They wash over me like a huge wave, sweep across my body, taking my body along with them; and the voices, which I can see! how strange, I can see sounds! gray, an undulating mass of tiny light-gray particles, but they are leaving my body behind, they're not taking it with them; they move on, across and through me; but it's not over yet, because fresh masses are coming, splashing across me, the mass of sounds makes me feel my body! here it lies under the ceaselessly cascading sounds, and I can see that this homogenous gray rumbling mass of sounds is made of the zigzagging of flashing sound fragments; but these flashing-glittering fragments, while they swoosh across me like a wave, appear as if they were in a mighty struggle among themselves, each trying to tear itself away from the grip of another, and then, out of two struggling ones a new sound, a new flash, is born; the one that got away! but then this third sound vanishes in the grayness of the mass, and it's no wonder, because each sound is like that, each one has to tear itself away from another, and each one is being shackled by another; the dying particles, vanishing into the gray mass, are emitting a great profusion of freed particles, which sparkle brightly, and every sparkle, every flash, shows itself to be different in the body of the rolling mass, and the refractions of each particle are also different as they all fall back down; up and down, they draw in their wake the pre-determined arcs of glittering bursts and cooling extinction, and the arcs intertwine, thus the unsystematic turns into a system and everything keeps moving forward.

I can see.

I can see the room. The bed, my legs, the strips of light blending into shadows through the glass of the open balcony door. And I can hear this profoundly light, lucid rumbling; the looping arcs, as they mingle with and leave one another in their race forward to a point which I cannot know because it is outside myself, it is beyond; I can see the sounds and I can see the room; the outside space and its reverberations inside, all at the same time; and I can see her body, standing in the waves of sounds; yes, these sounds, racing forward, sweep through her body, too, and she is standing within the rumbling, above me, and she is handing me the glass, but she doesn't seem to see the music.

She cannot see it. But I don't see it anymore either; it is receding, falling into the depths, like an avalanche; its receding rumbling sounds and its sight, however, leave the music for me; music in the silence, the music I can hear, music that organizes the infinity of silence into the strict yet playful order of finitude. And here she is, standing over me, with a glass in her hand. Every single sound of music is organized from silence, but it would not give itself back to silence; rather, it struggles, puts up a fight, and moves on, continues in another passage just so I won't notice that this single sound that has had an existence is now forced to expire; the sound that in its very continuity both denies and admits its own finitude; the next one, and the one after that, has also expired, fallen back into silence; yes, the ones that go on also expire and fall back, one after the other, because they each continue only in the fragment coming after it, on and on, and this is how the number increases of sounds that once existed, and this happens in so fast a succession that the speed itself, the pace, appears to deny its own matrix: the silence; yet silence still reigns between every two consecutive sounds; but the sounds try to move on so quickly, at such a pace, as not to allow this gap, this realm of silence between two single sounds, to expand, they want it to remain as narrow as possible! for each sound feels that if it does not continue, if the gap of silence widens, then it, the sound, must return to the place where it was born.

Then it's over. Then I've escaped, after all. Or is this a new motif, a new, recurring self-deception of temptation? No. Because music has just verified the problem I could not solve.

Time does exist, because there is forward progression, because there is a constant accumulation of whatever there was, or used to be.

But how does she know that she must verify something always at the point where I am about to reach my death? And then she yanks me back.

She is standing here above me. It's as if she's been standing here since the beginning of time, reaching out, handing me the glass. This cannot be true. It would be too beautiful, too sentimental, that it should be Mozart's music to awaken me to reality. A glass of water sparkling in the music, and the perfect features of her body. Too beautiful.

But the glass, though I didn't think it was a real glass, I can see; and my hands, my instincts, do take the glass from her hand, and I am already drinking the water. And over the rim of the glass I can see the anxious intentness of her face as it melts into a smile. I feel and hear the substance of the water as it runs down my throat in individual gulps, but I don't know where it goes from there; I seem to be but one large head with a huge emptiness beneath it, water drips into a void, though I see that there is a body there, the one gulping the water, I can see it exactly the way I see her body if I look over the rim of the glass, but now I must be very cunning, to deceive my own madness; drinking water is an automatism. I take the glass away from my mouth, even though I'd like to drink some more; this hot empty space, which is my head, would like some more water, but it's also possible that it desires not the water but the automatism of drinking, and that I cannot allow.

"Don't you want some more?"

"No."

"I'm very thirsty, too."

Above me, she is drinking what's left over. Her arm is stretched out, but it reaches somewhere which is outside the picture. Clink. The glass clinked. Yes. The night table is there, outside the visible picture, but if I turned my head I could see it. I do see it. And the tape recorder on top of the night table.

But why can't I hear the music?

I can, but it no longer touches me as it used to. In a great distance, beyond the realistically visible distance, on a bumpy road, music is jouncing forward, but where to? To get out of this impassive automatism of musical chords.

"Gimme a cigarette!"

I can hear my voice, but I've no idea how I thought of smoking a cigarette.

"I've smoked it. It's gone."

"When?"

"Just now. I've smoked it."

She's lying. She just says it so nothing will happen. So that I will stay in the automatism of sounds. Fall back into the place from which I've managed to extricate myself. So that this, too, should turn into a new motif, nothing but another round along my own circular course. There is no point in making accusations. That, too, would be only a repetition. At certain points these accusations are always repeated.

"My briefcase is there. I put it under the chair. You'll find a pack of cigarettes in my briefcase."

She gets up. How did I think of my briefcase? It flits across the picture I'm seeing now. It vanishes.

"I can't find it."

I lift myself up. It's as if I'm standing on the bed in an enlarged picture depicting the room. I make a move, it seems as if I'm flying among the objects: I cannot feel anything, I can only see. But the open balcony door is closed. Because I wanted to jump out again. But who closed it? It was open just a while ago.

Because I did want to jump out.

Cigarette between two fingers. I am smoking it, but I can't feel that

I am, I can only see it, and I can't taste it either. And when am I sitting here? Yes. Sitting here, with my back against the wall, on the bed, smoking, even though I don't want the cigarette. But this is not happening now, this is something that was. Silence is of the kind, I mean that silence is such, as to indicate that it is now that I'm sitting here, after all. The ashtray, yes, the ashtray is there, on top of the folder. So I am here, after all, because the radiator's only an arm's length away, and on the radiator is the folder on which I have my watch and two packs of cigarettes. I should take a look at the watch and then I'd know whether I am still sitting here or not. But for some reason, I don't know why, I am afraid; I'm scared to look at the watch, even though my hand is already there, now dropping the cigarette into the ashtray. But why are there two packs of cigarettes on the folder? There was only one before, the one torn open and empty, and now there is another one, too, and it's full. If there are two, that means I don't have to take a look at the watch, two means that time is moving on.

"Éva!"

"Yes, dear."

"Why are there two packs? How did the second one get there?"

"Do remember, dear. Try, always try to remember. I said the cigarettes were gone, because I smoked the last one. Remember? And then you got up, found your briefcase, after you looked for it for a long time, because you had put it under the chair but it was between the bed and the radiator. Do you remember? And you found it. You took that pack out of your briefcase. Remember?"

"I think I do, now that you mention it, it seems as if that's what happened, but maybe I'm just imagining it. But now we do seem to be really here, and having a conversation, though it sounds to me as if I'm again talking to myself."

"No. You're not talking to yourself, dear, you're talking to me."

"To you?"

"Yes."

"And you really are, really exist?"

"Yes, I really am here, with you."

"Then it looks like it's slowly going away, because it really feels like that to me, too, and I can really see that you are really here. I'd really love to have this thing go away."

"Of course it's going away. If only you'd try to sleep a little! That would be so good. Don't be afraid of anything, just try to sleep. That's all. If you'd try to remember, is it all right if I keep talking to you? it doesn't bother you? If you'd try to remember, you'd know that nothing's happened, we've only smoked, and what happened inside you is the effect of smoking, but this effect is going away, and you'll see the world again exactly the way it is. My talking doesn't bother you?"

"No. It's good to hear you talk, but don't go on!"

"Then try to sleep, dear. To sleep. You think you can go to sleep?"

"Yes. I believe

so; right now I feel as if I were ill and you're taking care of me. I confess, don't be angry, but I must confess, though I know I shouldn't, in a word, I don't know what illness I have, I only feel that I am ill. Maybe I've gone crazy, but that's just speculation, you know? I think I've completely lost my sense of time, though I had it; I do remember that I did, only I don't remember how good it was. Time has stopped, did you know that?"

"Do try to sleep, dear, all right? I'll turn off the light so it won't bother you, all right?"

There would be darkness if she turned off the light. But of course, the darkness! I have seen this room also as darkness; and then what is happening now is a repetition, or, more precisely, I can hear now what I should have heard then.

"No! Don't!"

We seem to have been talking. But then she should be here by my side. Where?

She is standing in front of the chest of drawers. Just now she seemed to be lying next to me, and we seemed to be talking, but now she is standing there, and she appears to be taking the clock in her hand.

"You see? I'm winding up the alarm clock, like this, turn after turn. I must wake up tomorrow morning because I have to go to work. Tomorrow? You see how silly I am! Time got all confused in me, too. Not tomorrow, today, because it's already past midnight. Well! There it is, all wound up. You see? It'll ring. Because, unfortunately, tomorrow will be a day like all the others up to now. And there is nothing wrong with time. Shall I tell you what time it is now?"

"No, don't! I don't want to know!"

"But I could tell you: half past twelve."

I can feel my compulsive movements. I can see how I am flailing my arms and kicking with my legs. I don't want to start from the beginning. I don't want to flail and kick, because these are also the movements of madness. But the anxiety attacks I can restrain only with the kicks of my will, and that makes me thrash about even more violently on the bed, and kick even harder, my arms flailing in larger and larger arcs. Because I don't want this to be happening.

"I'm turning off the light, all right?"

She is asking, or she has asked already. But if her voice is so calm, then what does it matter that I can see myself kicking and flailing, or that I feel that the very effort to resist is what makes my body alternately tense up and relax, causing all these insane movements; if her voice is this calm, that means she does not see what I see, that in reality I am lying motionless on the bed and only imagining all this.

"I'll turn off the light, all right?"

"All right."

Light or dark, it's all the same. Now it's dark. Then this is reality, after all; she's turned off the light, therefore it is dark in here. I'll get a good night's sleep and by morning everything will be the same as it used to be. No. I cannot sleep, because I have to be on guard. In the square of the window frame a glimmering gray light. Perhaps it is dawn already. Dawn is also a concept of time. That means I can't determine whether it exists or not. I close my eyes so I won't have to think about that. But the dark motionlessness is also in contact with time. Maybe I should go on waiting with my eyes open. Shouldn't be wanting anything. But if I don't want to want anything, that, too, is an activity of the will. And without will I cannot even give up. I should just submit, surrender. Doesn't matter to what. Whatever there is. My eyes got opened. I didn't want this to happen, still they got opened. That's how one should act, that's how one should behave. To let go: let whatever force work in me, and not be restrained by the force of will, because it would be useless anyway. It's dark. A night like all other nights. The light in the window frame is really gray, yet it's probably not the light of dawn but that of the streetlamps. There is no dawn. I was wrong. Or merely imagined it. Time is probably not moving forward. I should check the time now. My watch is within reach. I lift myself up so I can reach it, but in the meantime I feel I am not rising up at all but am still lying on the bed, just as I have been. I am sitting, but lying down. I'm lying on the bed on which I'm sitting, in the very same room which is now in darkness. But there is no such thing. It's impossible to sit and lie down at the same time. I should decide where I am now. Whether I am sitting on the bed on which I am lying down. One shouldn't decide anything. But then what is all this? The room is motionless and silent. It's nighttime. So I have fallen asleep. Or maybe I've been in some kind of stupor and just come out of it and can't remember the time that's gone by. This quilt I must have pulled over myself while I was asleep. That can't be, because a little while ago I was awake and this quilt wasn't here. I am holding it with my hand, so it's a real quilt. But even though I'm lying here, motionless, I feel as if I were groping around myself with quick, jerky little movements. If I could be free of these movements! I turn over to lie on my stomach. And I see that she is here, lying next to me. All rolled up, she is sleeping under the other quilt. But now she wakes, looks up at me, indifferent. Turns her quilt aside and gets up.

"Where are you going?"

She stands up.

"I'm cold. It got chilly in here. I'll get a quilt."

But why is she bringing a quilt when there is one here already? And it is warm. And there is a small pillow under my head. I don't know how it got there, under my head. She opens the door to the foyer. The door stays open and she disappears in the darkness of the foyer. That's where they keep the bedding, probably. But what kind of quilt is she going to bring if the quilt is already here? She appears in the darkened doorway with her arms pressing some large, white, shapeless thing to her body. She is coming toward the bed, letting some things slip from under her arms. Her arm seems to be swinging in my direction, and my body feels the weight, the touch of one of those things. Oh yes, the quilt, of course. She's thrown a quilt over me. And she is also holding out something toward me.

"Put this under your head."

But I'm unable to take it from her. I don't know why, I just can't. Her hand lifts my head and she slips that something under my head. In the dark I can see her face from very close up. A small pillow. But it's as if it isn't her in the darkness, and the face isn't hers either; the whole image simply reminds me of somebody.

My mother. Death. It's not that she was here, but it was her gesture: putting the small pillow under my head. And I can do it, too, prepare death just as my mother did. I'm not scared. Thought it over many times. I can get free only if I kill myself. All this is very simple. I can't feel my body now, can't feel anything. Which means I might stumble or swing over to the other side without being sure that I did, or maybe I'd do it while somehow also remaining on this side. But for sure, there will be a final moment when, without my being able to see it or feel it, all this ceases. The balcony door is closed. The room is bathed in the peaceful glimmer of scattered lights from outside. That's what's needed, a peaceful room like this, exactly. I am lying in bed, on my back. I still am. Above my head, somewhere outside, beyond the walls, the church bell strikes. And strikes again. Time. The time has come, thank you for the signal. But I'm lying on my stomach, the small pillow under my head. I turn around, sit up on the bed, but it seems as though I'm still lying down, on the same spot I've been lying on. But I don't really need the door! I can step out on the balcony through the window, too!

I am standing on top of the bed, so I must have stood up, but it still feels like I'm lying down, on my back; but I can see the enlarged picture, the picture which is nothing but a bird's-eye view of the darkened room: it's as if I'm standing on the bed in which I am lying down.

From here I can step on the windowsill. And I take the step. From here, from the windowsill, I can see the depth of the street under the dark stone balustrade of the balcony. The balcony is narrow, so I could just take off right from this windowsill. The street is empty. The balcony balustrade hides the pavement, only the gray shine of the windows across the street can be seen, and the round rose window in the massive block of the church, and the sidewalk down below; the pavement where I would crash cannot be seen! it's easy like that, and it's good to fall, because then you're between two places. Not yet there but no longer here either. And the thud, as if a heavy bundle of rags had been thrown down; but this was the thud of my own body! And in the silence I can hear approaching steps. Shouldn't have done it! But it's a good noise and

it's dark

and

then I am done with it, I'm over it, at last.

But if I'm over it,

why am I lying here? why am I imagining that the small pillow is here, if I'm not alive anymore. Or maybe I'm alive and only imagined that I died? And then it all continues. I can't stand it!

And why is it light now? If I only imagined death, why is the lamp turned on, why is the room light when it was dark just now? The room is light because she heard the thud of my body and she quickly turned on the light, only I'm not there anymore but here on the street, and I'm dead, only I can still see the room. She's sat up in the bed and is looking in the direction where the big wind is blowing from: the wind is tearing into and flapping her long blond hair; she thrusts her face into the wind and smiles, and I seem to hear her voice, too, though she isn't saying anything, her mouth isn't moving, only her body tautens, motionless, leaning into the howling wind; still, she seems to be speaking, calling me, by my name, but her mouth is not moving

"You will make it, dear. No problem. You'll make it. No problem. You'll make it."

this is not her! this is a hallucination! good, then I did die, after all! but if the same thing continues after death, why did I have to die? How should I get free of this death? It sure is dark. I'm lying on my stomach, in bed. I can see the large pillow, and her head on the large pillow, and she's asleep. And I can see the patterns in the wallpaper. This is what I should be looking at, these patterns. These patterns do not change, these are the patterns of the wallpaper. If I keep looking at them, no symbols of any kind will appear. But what sort of symbols am I thinking of? I simply had a dream, woke up, and am now lying here. What stupid dreams. If I look at these patterns, if I see only the edge of the big pillow and the wallpaper patterns, I can be sure I was only dreaming, then I woke up, and this is reality. But somehow it seems I haven't managed to wake up completely. As if the edge of the big pillow was not what I see it is but, rather, a hand. This can only be a dream. But it's not a dream because it is a hand. As if it weren't a real hand but a hand carved from wood. As if this carved, wooden hand were reaching toward me, because it was carved from a living tree that is reaching toward me to help me. The hand of Christ. Reaching for me. I must grasp it, since it has reached out for me. A dream. What a ridiculous dream. Still, I can feel I am not asleep. If I am not asleep, then Christ's hand cannot be a dream. If Christ reaches out to me like that, then I can't do what I had in mind. I must accept the hand because He's reaching out to me, to help me. Ridiculous. But as soon as I grasp it, the hand carved out of wood turns back into a big pillow. I let it go. But it's a hand again. No matter how I look at it or how suspicious I am, I can see a real, carved-wood hand reaching for me. Only I shouldn't touch it, because if I do, it disappears and pretends to be a big pillow. But if I don't touch it, if I don't hold it, I can't be sure whether it's a big pillow or the hand of Christ. It can't be the hand of Christ, because He is dead. But even if He is dead, He is reaching His hand toward me. After all, what I'm seeing is not a real hand but one carved from wood. Then He must want to take me to Himself, after all. And since He can no longer appear as real, He appears as a symbol. He wants me to die. I am not objecting, so why can't I die? Why must I still be living? Or, why is death here if I have to go on living? He probably knows. For sure, I no longer wish to wish for anything. I don't know how to want. I'm waiting. But for how long? How will I know for how long if I'm not allowed to know the time?

It is terrible to be waiting while in every single moment—and I never know whether any of these individual moments will pass at all—the whole of the present occurs, the present which may or may not exist at all. This is the situation, because I cannot know anything for sure. The large pillow is Christ's hand. This is only a motif. It fills out, stretches, and twists around time, which is motionless.

Later, I'm lying on my back, in bed. Covered with a quilt. I can feel it's later than it was before. I sit up. So, I am still here, in this room. I reach out, take my watch, turn it so that in the light coming from the street I can see its face. The small hand is almost on the three, the big hand is on the nine. I am looking at it. This means that it's a quarter to three. The thin second hand is also moving around the central axis. With lovely, even, nervous little jerks it clicks from its old place to its new one. But not forward. Only in a circle. Which is to say, not from its old place to its new place, but from its older place to its old one. Like a radius emanating from the center of a closed system. Round and round it goes. That is to say, it is repeating itself.

I am lying on the bed, and I know that a little while ago I wanted to sit up to take a look at the watch. But there's no need. It seemed to show, I seemed to have looked at it and it seemed to have shown that it was a quarter to three. Imagination. It can't show time. It keeps revolving around its own center exactly the way I do around mine.

Blue. Blue sky. Roofs. Light. Morning light on the rooftops. I sit up in bed. In the square of the window frame the blue sky and the morning light reflected by the rooftops. Outside, the sun is shining. But its light does not reach in here, into this room, the roofs hold it up, break it into umpteen fragments. She is sleeping right next to me, calmly, quietly. With her knees pulled up, under the quilt. She is wheezing quietly, evenly. Her head is sunk into the pillow. Her features are harsher than when she's awake. Her mouth is narrowed to a slit, as if in her dream she was wanting something. But it's a constant, even wanting, because her face, along with this wanting, is resting peacefully. If I can see this, if I can think about it like this, then perhaps nothing really happened. It was only a dream, I was simply dreaming. As if sensing that I've been watching her, her lids quiver and parts of her face also tremble a little around the mouth. Then she relaxes again, sinking back to where she had started from; but as if the sinking had scared her, her mouth quivers harder and so do her lids. She opens her eyes. Blue. How strange are blue eyes. She looks around disinterestedly, but how surprising it is to see her eyes; something which only a little while ago I couldn't see. Almost imperceptibly, her disinterest turns into attentiveness. She is alert, watching. First, only my face, then my body, my palm against the bed, then back to my face. She lingers on my face. If she pays this sort of attention, then everything must have happened. She says nothing, her attention deepens, growing somber. She stirs, sits up. The cover slips off her upper body.

Now I let the sight of her face go and look at her body: her neck, her breasts, each in turn, and her belly. The cover hides only her lap now. And I return to her face, too. It would be nice to touch her, feel her, hear her voice, talk to her, but I'm scared. I feel that this scrutiny has been going on so long, we can't stretch it out any longer. She jumps out of bed, but turns around. As if from this new position she could take a better, closer look at me. Then she quickly smooths out her long hair that has fallen into her face. She looks around.

"I'm thirsty."

The voice is artificially pained. She starts for the table. But the glass is not there.

She glances back. The glass is on the night table. Empty. She steps back. She lifts the glass to eye level. Looks through it. Puts it down. It clinks. Sits at the edge of the bed, lowers her head, her hair tumbles forward again. She sits like that for a long time. I can see only her spread-out buttocks and the bent arc of her spine, the smooth, brown, curving planes of her back. As if she were only a back, without a head. But she lifts her head and quickly slips back under the covers. She raises herself on her elbow. I can't watch her anymore. Behind her, swimming in the morning light, is a section of the room, exactly as much of the room as my field of vision can take in. I have already seen the room like this, on some other mornings. The table. The armchair. "Did the alarm go off?" "I don't know." "What time is it?" "I should be asking that." She smiles. "I slept really well. I think I'm all slept out." Her voice sounds high. "Éva!" "Yes, dear." Her voice goes into a higher pitch.

"I'm going. I don't feel like meeting them now." "Don't go, dear. I won't let them in here!" I can feel and see that I get up slowly, calmly: so this is not such a simple thing. My clothes are in and around the armchair. "It would be so nice if you stayed, dear." I pick up my pants, my shirt. But I can't find my underpants. "Yes, it would be." Of course, I didn't take off my underpants. I put on my shirt. And this is all very natural. I could wash up, at least wash my hands and face. Bathroom. Unfortunately, the mouthwash is gone. Towel, comb. Putting on the watch in the room. "Don't get up. It's still early. Sleep. You can sleep some more." "Shouldn't I ask when I'll see you again?" "You shouldn't!" Door. Quietly, so the little ones won't wake up. Another door. The door handle breaks off, stays in my hand. I'm looking at it. Put it down on the threshold. Staircase.

At the front door I am stopped by the street where I had crashed. I start off. Before turning the corner I look up at the balcony. Where she waits for me as I come around in the evening, and from where she waves to me when I leave. From where I crashed into the street, where I am now walking. I turn the corner. The sun shines into this street. People are coming and going, I am able to see, I can hear their steps. They are still few in number. It's still early. Time. I look at my watch, and feel the warmth of the sun on my back; half past five.

My shadow is walking ahead of me on the sidewalk. My shadow: head with ears, neck, shoulders, sharply foreshortened torso, the shadow of the feet shooting from the feet; in reality, my feet and my shadow-feet meet in my soles; the soles on which I'm walking, and therefore I can't see them, my shadow is gliding in front of me on the sidewalk. The movement of the legs is discontinuous. I am looking at my legs: bending at the knee, the moving leg swings forward, so that the weight of my body is on the other, motionless leg, but it is immediately followed by the other! and although the movement is continuous, its sections are clearly perceptible. The shadow of discontinuous movement is still continuous, a uniform gliding forward. The differences of continuity and discontinuity blend and merge only in my soles, in the weight of the body. My God, what idiocies one can think about! And nausea, I feel a mild nausea, too. But my shadow is gliding smoothly ahead of me. It cannot possibly feel my weight or the nausea, and yet it seems to be leading me. Where to? How long must I repeat these discontinuous movements of my legs? Is this repetition, this walking thing, another station? Station. That's a concept, an idea. God. Christ. Station. Very nicely I have returned to the old, well-known world of thinking, full of Christian concepts, and now with my legs I must keep repeating these discontinuous movements called walking until I reach the coffee shop where only last week I had a cup of coffee, because she forgot, yes, that day, too, she forgot to buy coffee, and yes, that day, too, we had a clear morning like this, and now I won't have to go on much longer with this leg-movement repetition, because I'm almost there, where I had coffee only last week, before taking the bus on Engels Square.